Weird Tales

SPRING 2009

SUBSCRIBE AT **WWW.WEIRDTALESMAGAZINE.COM**

WEIRD TALES was the *first* storytelling magazine devoted explicitly to the realm of the **dark and fantastic.**

Founded in 1923, WEIRD TALES provided a literary home for such diverse wielders of the imagination as **H.P. Lovecraft** (creator of Cthulhu), **Robert E. Howard** (creator of Conan the Barbarian), **Margaret Brundage** (artistic godmother of goth fetishism), and **Ray Bradbury** (author of *The Illustrated Man* and *Something Wicked This Way Comes*).

Today, O wondrous reader of the 21st century, we continue to seek out that which is most weird and unsettling, for your own edification and alarm.

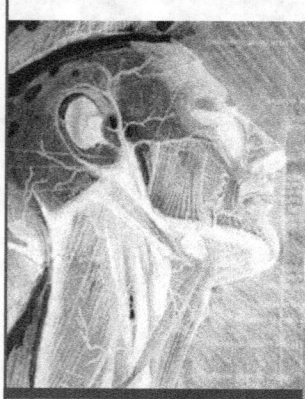

FICTION

POETRY

EDITORIAL & CREATIVE DIRECTOR Stephen H. Segal FICTION EDITOR Ann VanderMeer
CONTRIBUTING EDITORS Amanda Gannon, Kenneth Hite, Darrell Schweitzer
EDITOR EMERITUS George H. Scithers EDITORIAL ASSISTANTS Rae Bryant, Tessa Kum,
Colin Azariah-Kribbs CONTRIBUTING ARTISTS Steven Archer, Ira Marcks

PUBLISHER John Gregory Betancourt
ASSISTANT TO THE PUBLISHER Renee Farrah

All writers of such stories are prophets

FEATURES

H.P. LOVECRAFT'S HAUNT OF HORROR / BY RICHARD CORBEN / MARVEL COMICS

DEPARTMENTS

COVER ILLUSTRATION | *"Libra"* by Saara Salmi

VOL. 64, NO. 1 | **Issue 353**

WEIRD TALES ® is published 4 times a
year by Wildside Press, LLC. Postmaster
and others: send all changes of address
and other subscription matters to Wildside Press, 9710 Traville Gateway Dr.
#234, Rockville MD 20850–7408. Single
copies, $6.99 in U.S.A. & possessions; $10
by first class mail elsewhere. Subscrip-
tions: 4 issues $20 in U.S.A. & posses-
sions; $40 elsewhere, in U.S. funds.
Single-copy orders should be addressed to
WEIRD TALES at the address above.
Copyright © 2009 by Wildside Press, LLC.
All rights reserved; reproduction prohibited without prior permission. Typeset &
printed in the United States of America.
WEIRD TALES ® is a registered trademark owned by Weird Tales, Limited.

The eyrie

Goodbye to 85, Hello to the Future

BY STEPHEN H. SEGAL

Weird Tales might be the world's oldest speculative-fiction magazine, but here on the inside we feel like the youngest. We spent 2008, our 85th anniversary year, trying our damnedest to act as an ambassador for fantastical literature, reaching out to engage readers all across the diverse sub-circles of the modern geekosphere. Now we've learned that we've been named finalists for the Hugo Award for best semiprozine—the first Hugo nomination, incredibly, that *Weird Tales* has ever received. We're somewhat awed by the recognition, and we'd like to take this space to applaud the people who earned it.

For starters, there was you, our readers, who answered our public call to name "The 85 Weirdest Storytellers of the Past 85 Years" with more correspondence than any other project in the twenty years since *Weird Tales*'s resurrection. You helped us craft an unprecedented portrait of the modern imagination, detailing the web of bizarre ideas and aesthetics that linked Philip K. Dick to Andy Warhol, Laurie Anderson to Madeleine L'Engle, and H.P. Lovecraft to Frida Kahlo to that German guy who founded the "Body Worlds" exhibit.

Of course, the undying heartbeat of *Weird Tales* remains the tales themselves, and 2008 was quite a year for our stories. Fiction editor Ann VanderMeer could have sat back and enjoyed the accolades for acquiring an all-new Elric novella by Michael Moorcock, an original sword-and-sorcery battle by Norman Spinrad, an unforgettable dark-superhero story by Tim Pratt, the return to short fiction of Kathe Koja, two brilliantly disparate pieces by O. Henry Award

winner Karen Heuler (a comedy with fish and an allegory with beetles), and an all-international issue with stories from Serbia, Spain, Israel, Singapore, the Netherlands, Slovakia, and the Philippines. But instead, Ann delighted in introducing readers to an onslaught of newer writers who are sure to become some of tomorrow's superstars. We saw the likes of Ramsey Shehadeh's post-apocalypic fable "Creature"; Chris Furst's twisted history "The Last Great Clown Hunt"; Micaela Morrissette's culinary hallucination "Wendigo"; Chiles Samaniego's jazz-club folktale "Time and the Orpheus"; Rachel Swirsky's passionate dream-scene "Detours on the Way to Nothing"; and Matthew Pridham's stunning first sale "Renovations," a haunted-house novelette told in the first person by the house itself.

All these stories had to be illustrated, naturally, and *Weird Tales* was thrilled to introduce a wave of fantastic young artists to the American SF scene in 2008. Issue #348 gave us the unsettlingly seductive fish-women of Finnish artist Saara Salmi, while #350's straightjacketed jester marked the cover debut of Jason "Stuntkid" Levesque. Our anniversary issue's cover saw a raw, punk-rock vision of Elric of Melniboné, courtesy of Newel Anderson; edgy pen-mistresses Star St. Germain and Molly Crabapple gave us werewolves in sun-dresses and rock stars in goblin suits; and comics artist Ira Marcks introduced us to the esoteric wares of Harvey Pelican & Co. Meanwhile, online at WeirdTalesMagazine.com, mixed-media artist (and musician) Steven Archer undertook a quest to create an original Lovecraftian work every day from one Balticon to the next.

It was a fantastic anniversary celebration, and now it's over. But the *Weird Tales* renaissance, we hope, has only just begun. Keep an eye out for lots more excitement in the coming year—ranging from a truly *unique* steampunk special to an all-new online series of original micro-fiction. Please, stick around and stay weird with us! ☙

THE GREATEST POISON

Caught by the death magic of J.G. Ballard

I HAVE A FAIRLY embarrassing confession to make: I've never done drugs. Okay, so I've been drunk to the point of oblivion on more than one occasion. And I'm sure I've copped a contact high once or twice in my life. Then there's the time I ate a single chocolate-covered mushroom while on tour with a friend's band and partying after a concert in Omaha. The mushroom, though, had no effect. Not even a stomachache. Timothy Leary would have been so disappointed in me.

Maybe it's because I grew up in a household where drugs were enjoyed openly and unapologetically, but they've never held much mystique for me. No aura of otherness. No magic. I've always looked to things other than drugs to blow my mind, to stretch my senses, to reupholster my reality. Specifically, I've looked to art: music, comics, movies, books. I remember hearing Syd Barrett for the first time around the age of 17 and wondering how a human brain could rewire itself so enchantingly. Bob Burden's impish *Flaming Carrot* comics proved to me the absurdity of normalcy and the fascism of logic. And a steady diet of the Davids Lynch and Cronenberg gave me vivid visions of the weirdness that fluttered just under the skin of the universe. It wasn't mushrooms, but it seemed to do the trick.

But the most radical artistic hallucinogen I've ever consumed—the greatest poison, from the hand of the greatest pusher—is the fiction of J.G. Ballard.

When J.G. Ballard died of cancer on April 19 at the age of 87, literature lost one of its sharpest and most surgical minds. Ironically, it also lost one of its most fervid, feverish shamans of the psyche. "Psyche-

delic," however, is not a word usually associated with Ballard's work. From his post-apocalyptic novels of the '60s to his stranger (yet somehow more mundane) dystopias of the '70s and beyond, his fiction has always been discussed, and often dismissed, in a drizzle of pat adjectives that include dry, dispassionate, clinical, cerebral, analytical, even antiseptic.

Those modifiers, overused as they've been, are dead on. And yet they couldn't be more wrong. Ultimately, Ballard's prose—for all its ostensible detachment from, you know, humanity and emotion and all that—is some of the most messily, magically human writing that the world of speculative fiction has ever produced.

My first exposure to Ballard was his collection of science-fiction short stories, *Chronopolis*, which I read in high school. I was a smartass punk at the time—in fact, a few well-placed bongs hits might have done me a world of good—who'd just latched onto the bleak, ascetic music of Joy Division. While reading old articles about the band, I learned that their song "The Atrocity Exhibition" had been named after a book by someone named J.G. Ballard. This was pre-eBay, so I had no real way to track down this Ballard person's stuff

Ballard was among our most fervid, feverish shamans of the psyche.

other than at the library or a used bookstore. (Ballard has been, and probably always will be, sadly underrepresented on the shelves of booksellers). *Chronopolis* wound up being the first Ballard book I ran across—so, out of curiosity, I plunked down three bucks for it. I took it home. I might have even put on Joy Division's "The Atrocity Exhibition."

Then I read it.

It freaked me the fuck out.

Up to that point I'd been a fan of writers like Stephen R. Donaldson, John Varley, Roger Zelazny. Most trafficked in altered states of one kind or another. Still I'd never heard of, let alone read, science fiction as bizarre as Ballard's. A giant's body washed up on a beach, only to be gradually dissected and desecrated by the Lilliputians that are, really, us? Sleep-deprivation experiments that distort the way its subjects intersect spacetime itself? It felt as though a small portion of my brain, dormant my whole life, had woken and begun ingesting the rest of it.

The next Ballard book I devoured was the 1966 novel, *The Crystal World*, which remains my favorite of his. As I'd later figure out, it marks the transition between his early, formative body of work to his mature period: in other words, a pubescent novel for a pubescent me. Accordingly, *The Crystal World* portrays an Earth in the throes of some quantum puberty, a frantic yet inexorable transmutation of all terrestrial matter from green, warm, and mushy to clear, cold, and crystalline.

I didn't know what magic realism was back in high school. In fact, I'm sure I'd never heard that term. As an adult I've come to adore the works of Gabriel García Márquez, Jorge Luis Borges, and Italo Calvino, not to mention brilliant new practitioners of the form like Kelly Link and Benjamin Rosenbaum. But now, in hindsight, I see J.G. Ballard's work—particularly *Chronopolis*' "The Drowned Giant" and his '70s novels *High-Rise, Concrete Island,* and *The Unlimited Dream Company*—as being not only psychedelic in their own way, but utterly magic realist, possessing of an almost folktale-like sense of wonder, of heightened probability and perception.

Granted, magic realism and psychedelia have plenty in common. Both can range in tone from idyllic to horrific—and often do in the span of a heartbeat. Both seek to distill and mingle the real and the unreal. And, at their root, both aim to shroud phantas-

magoria in an unbroken aura of reality, of ontological integrity. Take Ballard's 1974 novel *High-Rise*: In it, life in an upscale tower block morphs into a brutal, tribal existence that culminates in everything from incest to cannibalism. What sparks such a fantastic metamorphosis? In a typical science fiction tale, it would be a mutant virus, a government experiment, or some other stock trope. In *High-Rise*, the explanation is paradoxically far more prosaic and far more fantastic: Such a perversion of modern life is simply the ultimate and inevitable evolution of modern life—technocracy swallowing its own tail.

Even more insidious, though—and this is fundamental to the understanding of Ballard as a magic realist—is the fact that none of the residents of his terrific high-rise seek to escape their nightmare existence. They don't lose their intelligence. They don't forget about the world outside (which, by the way, remains presumably untouched by this madness, **>>>**

The Library

Book Reviews | BY CRAIG LAURANCE GIDNEY

FANTASIES *of the* SENSES

Lush otherworldliness from Catherynne M. Valente and Tanith Lee

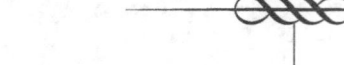

PALIMPSEST
by Catherynne Valente
(Spectra, trade paperback, $14)

PALIMPSEST IS A magical city that exists on the border between dream and reality. Part Hieronymus Bosch painting, part steampunk wonderland, the cities wonders and terrors enchant all who visit; it seems to echo all of their wildest wonders and terrors. Visitors from our world can only access it one way: through sex with those similarly affected (infected?) by their visit. After their visit, travelers are marked with a tattoo—a map of the section of the city they first explored. The city exudes a kind of portmanteau magic—it seems attuned to psyches of its tourists. There are wild, living trains that traverse the city on their own schedules. Kanji are born out of cabbages, mechanical insects prowl the air and a river of eggwhite flows through it. The denizens are often animal headed, victims and veterans of a recent war. Palimpsest is kept under the watchful and sometimes cruel eye of Casmira, creator of the insects.

The novel follows four of the most recent visitors to the city. All four are damaged in unique ways. Sei is a bluehaired girl from Kyoto, obsessed with trains and haunted by the memory of her mad mother. Ludovico is an Italian bookbinder, searching for his wife, who has disappeared in Palimpsest. Beekeeper November lives in isolation in the Bay Area, while émigré locksmith Oleg wishes to find his dead sister's ghost. *Palimpsest* weaves their complicated, tortured tales in episodic bursts through a travelogue of the city. These disparate threads eventually form a plot, as each of them seeks to immigrate to Palimpsest permanently.

Valente's real-life scenes are written in an oblique, impressionistic style. She chooses the imagery of her characters carefully, and they aren't exactly likeable; each of them is blocked in some way. Some of them go to hellish extremes to achieve their aims. But the flawed characters are real, human, and their connection to the city makes sense. The travelogue sections are pure poetry. Valente's imagination is a boundless thing, coming up with enough ideas to fuel 1000-page fantasy novels. The sex scenes, which are frequent and include threesomes and same sex couplings, are never gratuitous. The sex scenes transcend mere eroticism, and have an alchemical quality. It's as if Anais Nin wrote Italo Calvino's *Invisible Cities*.

Palimpsest, with its phastasmorgia, willful obscurantism and oblique language, is not for everyone. But for those like more esoteric fiction, it's a must have.

TEMPTING THE GODS: THE SELECTED STORIES OF TANITH LEE, VOL. 1
by Tanith Lee
(Wildside Press, hardcover, $24.95)

TANITH LEE IS one of the modern masters of the weird tale, and this collection, the first of a two-volume series, brings together her fiction from the sixties to the late nineties. They range in genre from high fantasy to science fiction, and in tone from morbidly humorous to darkly horrific. All the pieces display her trademark language, vivid imagery and ominous wit.

While not a strictly themed anthology, many stories in this collection of Lee's work do deal with divinities and deities. The specter of Kore (Persephone) haunts the players in "Death Loves Me," set in ancient Greece. The goddess of death and spring appears in various forms in this complicated tale of a merchant's wife and a charioteer's eventual meeting. The science fictional "Ondralume" juxtaposes a drought cursed world's plea to the gods, with the rather surprising life of the gods themselves. "God and the Pig" is a philosophical dialogue between the titular characters in world overrun with pollution and social decay, while the Arthurian tale "The Kingdoms of the Air" concerns the emotional and spiritual cost of religious relic questing.

The other stories exhibit Lee's terrific range. The dark, psychosexual "Cain" will make your skin crawl. The Arabian Nights-styled "These Beasts" has a swashbuckling tale that could have come out of the Golden Age. "After I Killed Her" is a dragon tale with a Lee twist, and "Where Does the Town Go at Night?" ends the collection on a deeply disquieting note.

Tempting the Gods is an excellent introduction to the work of one of the masters of fantastic fiction. The second volume, *Hunting the Shadows*, will be published later this year. ✪

WEIRDISM *(continued)*

>>> at least for the time being). Dulled by the tyranny of social authority, they just... go with the flow. In a sense, there is a mutant virus at work in Ballard's novels—but rather than pathogenic, his viruses are invaders of the wholly metaphysical variety.

Ballard's cool, calm, collected delirium rocked my adolescent world. Barrett? Burden? *Blue Velvet*? They couldn't touch Ballard. Like I said, I grew up surrounded by drugs. Even as a little kid, I saw firsthand the casual madness and abandon adults could exhibit while under the influence. It came as no surprise to me to learn that Ballard himself attributed much of his worldview to his childhood. His of course, was far more extreme than mine. As detailed in his semi-autobiography, *Empire of the Sun*, and later in his proper memoir, *Memories of Life*, Ballard witnessed the almost artful barbarism humans were capable of as a boy in China during the Japanese occupation of World War II. The fact that he studied medicine as a young man only seems to reinforce his image as a literary clinician—but, taken as a whole, Ballard's formative years and his body of work constitute a thing of warped and disgusting beauty, sculpted from raw psychic pulp and tatters of reality.

When I read Ballard, I don't feel cold. No existential chill. No distance. I feel viscera slapped against my forehead, pubic hair in my teeth, lymph running down my chin. It's *all* viscera, all emotion. Only instead of going about it slapdash or scattershot like too many authors of the fantastic, Ballard doles his out in rigorous doses. Hypodermically, even. And his shit? It's pure. "Take my hand and I'll show you what was and will be," intones Ian Curtis at the end of "The Atrocity Exhibition," one of the most doom-laden moments in Joy Division's infamously somber oeuvre. And, in essence, that's what the death magician J.G. Ballard did to me at the age of 17, my brain already afire with hormones and a deep skepticism of the appearance of existence. He took my hand. He showed me what was. He showed me what will be. And he still does. ✪

Jason Heller is a Denver-based journalist and speculative fiction writer whose work has appeared in *The Onion A.V. Club*, *SF Weekly*, and *Westword*, among many other venues.

Steampunk Etc. | BY AMANDA GANNON

BELOVED DARKNESS, OBSCURE ODDITIES

The fantasy art duo of Bethalynne Bajema and Myke Amend

I**T IS THE SORT** of portrait that once graced turn-of-the-century postcards, featuring women from exotic lands. This woman's strange eyes are in sharp focus, promising just a hint of danger; the rest is hazy, dreamlike, uncertain. She wears a stylish vest that appears modern, but what at first looks like an elaborate hairstyle resolves upon further examination into a headdress reminiscent of horns. Her lips are faintly blue, and her jewelry dangles with well-crafted insects. Real as she seems, there's little natural about this woman; she is an otherworldly Ziegfeld girl, romantic and dangerous, sitting for some diabolical portraitist.

That portraitist is Bethalynne Bajema, whose recent *Sepia* series offers a spectrum of such darkly fantastic portraits of beautiful women. Some stare with disconcerting eyes of silver or blank white or solid black. Some look away, engulfed in a dreamlike fugue. Draped in flowing cloth, they wear masks and headdresses that evoke flowers, bat wings, tentacles. An element of the Nouveau hovers about them—as well as a hint of punk, a thoroughly modern surrealism, and just a touch of the pinup artist's tongue-in-cheek. It's a wonderful combination: dreamlike, romantic, and quietly unsettling.

"It's a shame that so many people only associate blue skies and singing birds with happiness and beauty," Bajema says. "A stormy sky against green trees is just as beautiful, and that's what makes me feel happy. I like things that are dark and beautiful, not necessarily bad or evil, but that have an uncertain overtone." She achieves this captivating ambiguity by combining stylistic techniques: scanning photographs, digitally altering them, printing them, altering them on paper, scanning them again, and so forth, shaping layer upon increasingly phantasmagoric layer.

Bajema acknowledges that she's been particularly drawn to steampunk and neo-Victorian themes of late—"but to me, my work still falls under the dome of simple fantasy." And while she cites influences including fantasy artist Brom and her mentor, neo-symbolist photographer John Santerineross, Bajema's ongoing creative companion is fellow artist Myke Amend. A decade of long-distance friendship between two professionals became a true partnership when they met in person at a horror convention, and the two have been artistically inseparable ever since.

A ROBOTIC HOLY MAN stands before a field of cold pipework crosses, black duster billowing. A superimposed halo of gears and dials surrounds him, he holds a clockwork bible in one hand while the other reaches for the steampunk pistol at his hip. Lengthy examination reveals an almost-hidden skull in the background—the only truly organic detail—and an oncoming train.

The image itself is a digital composition by Myke Amend. As in much of his art, the "preacherman" theme is obvious, but this piece's specific meaning grows more ambiguous the longer one stares at it. Amend's work is often complicated, like the man himself: an experimenter in music, computer programming, website design, writing, and art of all kinds. Growing up, he was as steeped in the fantastic, brooding elements of '80s and '90s metal and early gothic rock as in the graphic artists who defined that era: Frazetta, Riggs, Whelan, Brom. It seems only natural that Amend doesn't work in any single medium, but plays with everything from ink to

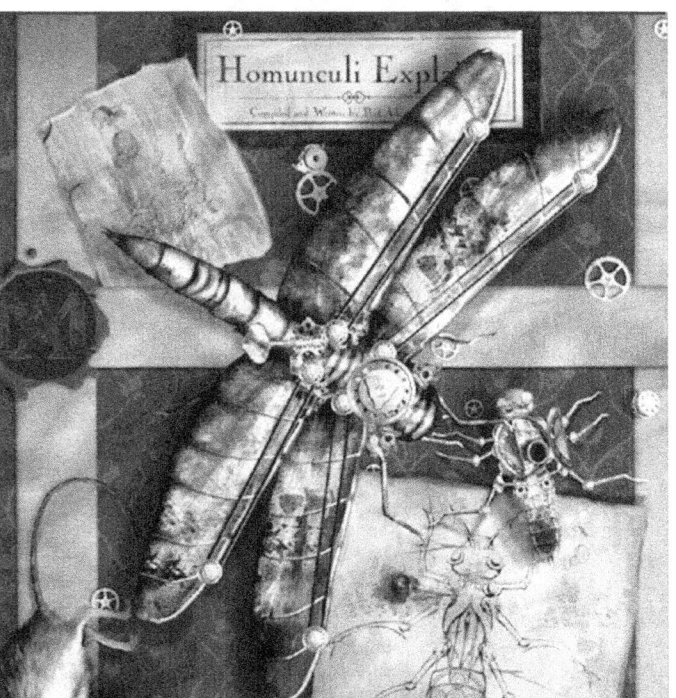

acrylics to digital manipulation. Strangeness and obscurity fascinate him: "Even the brightest and happiest things have a way of slipping off into the lower planes of Hell by the time they are completed," he says, "as if my hands are posessed by some great and ancient evil."

This combination of style and darkness has made Amend popular with the counterculture crowd. He has created commissioned work for the steampunk bands Abney Park and Vernian Process; his art is owned by Kaja Foglio of *Girl Genius* comics fame, by musician/artist Voltaire, and by other luminaries of the goth and steampunk scenes.

Amend's latest project is a dark humor comic: *Some Ghouls Wander By Mistake.* There's much more the artist would like to accomplish in the years to come—but above all, he wants to contribute to the aesthetic that has inspired him, and to continue seeking out new inspirations every day. "I suppose this is one of many things that serve to keep me young. This and bathing in clown's blood, of course." ☉

Bethalynne Bajema and Myke Amend have created the Miskatonic Archive, an online resource for fiction, art, news, and events with a particularly Lovecraftian steampunk spin, at miskatonicarchive.com. Their work can also be found at bajema.com, mykeamend.com, and ettadiem.com.

CARROUSEL VARIETY

HARVEY PELICAN & CO., Favorite Unlikely Supply House on Earth, Ipswich.

Manical Musements
SOMETHING WICKED
FOR SUSPICIOUS CHILDREN

The following selections are from the series "Animal Wars"

"CHARMED."

PLAGUE·FROG·3   MEDIC·PELICAN   BABOON·BRUTE   ALLIED·SEAHORSE

STEALTH·CRAB   BANNER·MAN   PLAGUE·FROG·7   QUAIL·VIPER   SHEEP·TRANSPORT

"FOR THE TOTS."

SUFFERING ELEPHANT
musical selection
44 East 25th St.
♪ "They BELLOW BELOW stage."

MANIPULATION OR ANIMATION OF CAROUSEL "SEATS" BY PERSONS OF MAGICAL PERSUASION IS STRICTLY PROHIBITED.

TIME TRAVEL IS NOT A FEATURE OF OUR CAROUSEL SYSTEMS.

AVAILABLE IN CRANK + STEAM.

ADMIT IT. HARVEY SAYS YOU WANT ONE.

You're a Stain

BY MICHAEL PHILLIPS

1
She's on you now, her legs straddling your waist,
your back to a hard kitchen floor.
You struggle under her weight, but it's no use, she has you.

2
Her legs are pale, cold, unyielding.
Her skirt is short, black leather.
Her shirt is white, clinging wet and sticky to her body, stained red.
Stained with what?

3
She wants you so badly, she aches for you.
She wants you, she wants you inside her, deep and forever.
You don't want to go, but you have no choice, never did.
You're hers.

4
She leans in close, her long black hair tickles your face.
Her lips touch your neck, cracked and icy.
Her teeth sink into your throat, teeth tearing flesh,
warm blood pooling around your head.
It's a kiss like you've never had, never wanted.

5
You're inside her now.
The rest of you, just another stain.

Michael Phillips is a writer from Tampa, Florida. The written word, to him, is like fine art, like liquor, beautiful and intoxicating. He'll tell you writing's possibly the only thing he does well, which is probably true. Due to the magic of bad genetics he doesn't walk, nor does he breathe without the assistance of machines. One could also argue that he's simply astonishingly lazy. Michael also doesn't speak due to a little breathing tube in his throat; thus Johnny Depp once played his voice on an Emmy-award-winning episode of Showtime's *This American Life*. Michael writes something akin to a live memoir at lithiumcreations.com, as well as short fiction. At night, he's a disco goddess.

ILLUSTRATION BY FRENTA

THE WEIRD TALES INTERVIEW

THOMAS LIGOTTI

*Geoffrey H. Goodwin asks horror's offbeat genius:
must life be so very decayingly crummy?*

I F YOU'RE A *newcomer to* Weird Tales, *know now that on a short list next to Edgar Allan Poe and H.P. Lovecraft, Thomas Ligotti is one of the finest writers of depressed and deranged narrators ever to have picked up a pen.*

His bleak fictive world is well depicted in three recent releases: Teatro Grottesco, *a collection of some of the author's finest work;* The Nightmare Factory, *a two-volume graphic novel adapting stories from his book of the same name; and* The Frolic, *a film version of his short story. Ligotti's freshly re-released*

short novel My Work is Not Yet Done *stands as further testament to his dark oeuvre.*

"Ligotti has screated an interconnected landscape of dread," artist Harry O. Morris has said, "by disallowing logic and psychological time, and by creating twisting cardboard sets with puppet characters." That landscape provides the setting for this new Weird Tales Interview, as Ligotti brings together his thoughts on Poe, rejecting life, crafting weird stories, and his yet-unpublished work of dark philosophy, Conspiracy Against the Human Race.

Have all great horror writers been alien to society? That would depend on one's idea of what makes a great horror writer as well as how willing one is to make an incredibly sweeping generalization. My personal preference has always been for writers who may or may not move about with ease in society but who at bottom are hostile not only to any conceivable social order, but also to being a member of the human race. Of course, this attitude is difficult for anyone, writer or not, to sustain on a daily basis. It would be more like a pilot light glowing inside one that occasionally flares up into a conflagration. Among the throng, it would be a non-adaptive aberration. No parent would hand his or her child a collection of Poe's tales and say, "Kid, this is how things are in this world. Attend particularly to 'The Man of the Crowd' and its epigraph from La Bruyére: 'This great misfortune—the inability to be alone.'"

Is all of life more trouble than it's worth? This is a question that each of us must answer on our own. It's probably best addressed at the hour of death, when an individual can survey how much trouble he went through and what he got for it. But even then our perspective is not without prejudice. To make an earlier judgment on whether or not life is more trouble than it's worth is certainly everyone's prerogative. The trouble is, whatever you conclude is not provable. There is no way to tally what makes life worth living, or what makes someone think that life is worth living, and measure this against what makes life not worth living. In one of his letters, Lovecraft wrote that life is worth living for one-third of the human race, not worth living for one-third of the human race, and neither one way or the other for the remaining one-third. Positive psychologists claim that eighty percent of us are happy with our lives, or at least are happy with our lives so far. Then there is the view that most of us lead lives of quiet desperation, and sometimes not so quiet desperation. None of these figures, or any others, seems dependable.

Do you think that your stories are connected to each other? I think they're thematically connected in their pessimistic view of existence. Beyond that, I'm probably not in the best position to judge.

Why do some readers want to be terrorized by their imaginations? There aren't any readers who want to be terrorized by their imagination. They want to be entertained or, to put it another way, they want to be stimulated. And some people are entertained and stimulated by depictions of the gruesome or the strange. Rare are the readers who, beyond being entertained and simulated, actually derive some kind of satisfaction and even comfort because they recognize an author's terrifying vision of reality as their own, or something close to it, and feel gratitude that someone else has given expression to that vision. It works the same way for all readers whose vision of the world is supported by that of literary works, which are often perceived as having a certain authority much like that of religious scriptures.

You've said that you've always loved writers who are underachievers. Who has generated the least output and is worth reading? By "underachiever" in the world of literature I mean those who really have to be motivated to produce a work and can do so only under certain conditions. These writers don't write because they are addicted to writing and believe that practically every idea they have for a story or a poem is an idea worth developing to its conclusion. A. E. Housman, the author of the classic *A Shropshire Lad*, published only three collections of poems over a lifetime of around seventy years. He said that he could write only during protracted periods when he was slightly depressed. In his fifty-one years, Bruno Schulz wrote only during what he called "unpolluted time" when he wasn't distracted by everyday considerations, mostly the need to earn a living. His main work ex-

ists in two slim collections of short stories, although he is also supposed to have written a novel, one that I would bet is also a slim work. One of the great modern underachievers in the horror genre is T.E.D. Klein, who as fiction writer has published a novel, a masterful collection of four novellas, and a small collection of stories which contains his masterpiece, "The Events at Poroth Farm."

I should say that even before I began writing and became a literary underachiever myself, I was a fan of underachievers. I'm not saying that my stories are worth reading, but only one of them, "The Frolic," was written under peculiar circumstances and during times of hyper-motivation.

Did you see the Tim Burton *Sweeney Todd*? Yes, I did. If you're not familiar with the original production of Sondheim's musical, I believe you would have good reason to think well of Tim Burton's truncated rendition. I'm one of those people who feel that what was left out of the movie version was to its severe detriment.

What is the current wallpaper on your computer? A photograph of boarded-up, abandoned house on the east side of Detroit.

Is *Conspiracy Against the Human Race* a form of weird nonfiction? How did it come into existence? *Conspiracy Against the Human Race* had its origins in a long interview I did several years ago. As it now stands, the book that evolved doesn't much resemble that interview except in spirit. *Conspiracy* interweaves several thematic threads and ultimately resolves into a view of human existence as an ordeal resembling those depicted in tales of supernatural horror. Like certain of these narratives, the book proceeds toward a revelation that we are not what we think we are, a conclusion that in some way parallels that of Lovecraft's "Facts Concerning the Late Arthur Jermyn and His Family," in which the title character discovers that he is the descendant of a tribe of white apes and this news becomes the impetus for his committing suicide. While most of us wouldn't set ourselves on fire upon finding out that we had the blood of white apes coursing through us, this revelation is too much for Arthur Jermyn. It seems to him an abomination and an unbearable violation of his sense of himself.

In *Conspiracy*, the abomination is the birth of human consciousness, a mutation that we do everything in our power to ignore because it reveals to us some things, such as death, that we cannot integrate into our lives, even if we are morticians. This self-protective ignorance means that we live in a permanent state of bad faith, a mutual misrepresentation of ourselves to one another for the sake of remaining sane and following our biological imperative to continue as a species. The only remedy for this situation, should we ever acknowledge it on a global scale, would be allow ourselves to become extinct. We are fraudulent beings—puppets, so to speak—who do not know themselves as such. The basics of this idea are taken from the works of the Norwegian philosopher Peter Wessel Zapffe as well as other thinkers who have concluded that conscious life is an accident or mistake in addition to being far more awful than we can ever admit it is.

Of course, none of us will choose to go extinct because we are not who we think we are—ask any philosophical determinist or neuroscientist who believes that we dance to forces beyond our control. And none of us will choose to go extinct no matter how awful some pessimistic spoilsport contends our lives to be. But the point of *Conspiracy* is not to persuade anyone to join the cause for humanity's discontinuance. Such an aim would be unrealistic at best. The point of *Conspiracy* is to convey my personal sense of the effectively supernatural horror of existence, a horror that closely relates to why some characters in horror stories would rather kill themselves than live with what they know.

In "The Last Feast of Harlequin," the first story I wrote that I considered a keeper, the main character is a depressive who discovers that his condition signifies something far worse than he suspected. At the end, he announces his intention to kill himself, perhaps by self-immolation or possibly by some other means.

This year being the bicentenary of the birth of Edgar Allan Poe, I'd like to ask what you admire about Poe's work. As a reader and a writer, your bent seems to be toward works with a definite supernatural orientation, something that is not found in abundance in Poe. It's true that Poe's horror stories don't really focus on supernatural elements in any major way. They are tales of madness, violence, and pain. But they do take place in a world that is wholly evil, desolate, and suffused with a profound sense of a doom without a name. This is what makes him the greatest of all horror writers. There is just nothing worth living for in Poe's world, and if there seems to be an object of desire in his theater of demented puppets, it turns out to be an object of horror.

The world of Poe's tales doesn't represent the so-called real world. One never has the sense that anything exists outside the frame of his narratives. I remember that when I read Kafka's *The Trial*, I was jarred when an Italian businessman makes a brief appearance. I thought it a mistake for Kafka make this reference to the normal world when everything else in *The Trial* takes place in wholly enclosed, abnormal world. In Poe, the reader is enclosed in such an environment. This enclosure is perhaps the secret of atmosphere in works of horror, because by this technique a writer can come as close as possible to conveying the feeling of a dream, which has no correspondence in waking life. When you dream, you don't feel that anything exists that is not in your immediate surroundings.

Then there is the fundamental strangeness of dreams, and I think Poe's stories also reflect this phenomenon. While you're read-

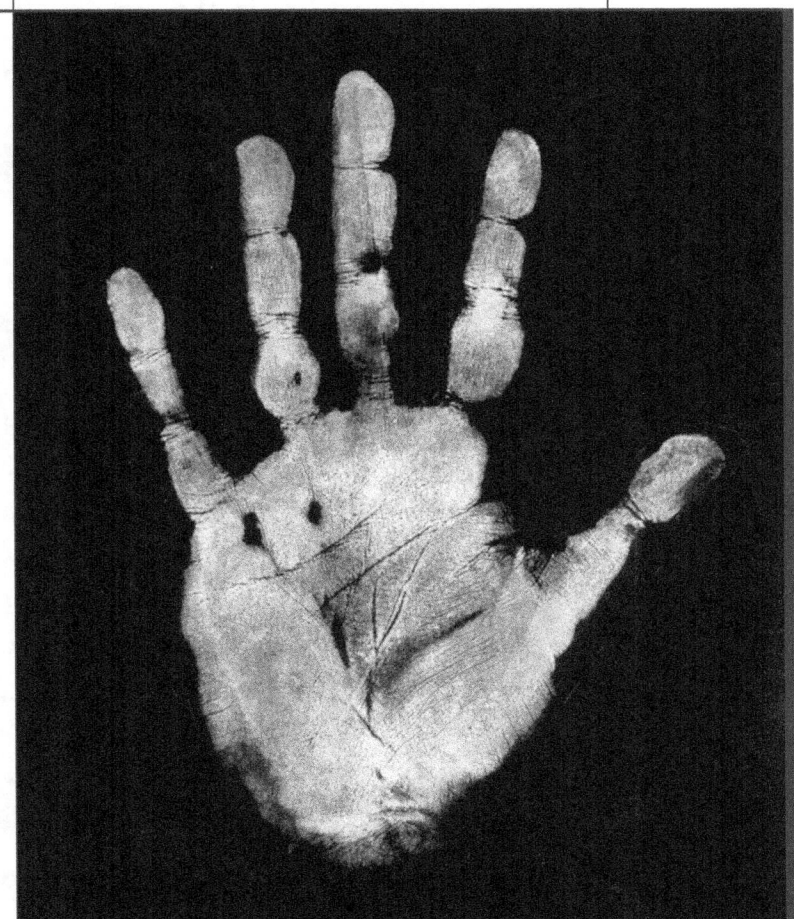

ILLUSTRATION BY FOTOGISÈLE

ing "The Tell-Tale Heart" or "The Fall of the House of Usher" you have a general sense of nightmarish events unfolding, but you don't feel that you're following a sequence of incidents that is wildly incoherent at the time. Only afterward might it occur to you that there are some unanswered questions and a mystery at the heart of these narratives. There are just no explanations that are sufficient to allow you to dispense with these narratives, which is what makes them so enduring. They've gone past all the superficial rationality that adequately holds the world together for us on a day-to-day basis and hit bottom where logical explanations end. All great stories have this element of impenetrable mystery, but in the genre of horror fiction this is a rare thing. Horror writers seem to feel that if they don't explain everything they'll lose the reader and their stories will be failures.

You've said: "Until I attained some recognition for my horror stories I could barely stand to live with myself." Having won substantial awards and been published around the world, did it actually change the experience of living with yourself? Yes it did. When Harry Morris's Silver Scarab Press came out with my first collection, *Songs of a Dead Dreamer*, I felt I had gotten something out of my system. What I wanted to be was one of those horror writers who publish a single collection of stories that finds a place on the shelves of aficionados of supernatural fiction. Later I aimed higher, setting my sights on being a flash in the pan—one of those writers who produce a work that attracts notice for a short time but who never again equals that one achievement. I never imagined that I would end up attaining the status of a cult horror writer. That's not something you can try to do. It just has to happen through some mysterious process.

Your work has a timeless and universal quality, but is being embraced by newer forms of pop culture, with "The Frolic" being made into a film and two volumes of illustrated retellings coming out as comics. What is it like for older stories to find new lives? I once read that J. D. Salinger has a legal blockade against any film adaptation of *The Catcher in the Rye* as long as he or his estate owns the rights to the book, which will be for quite a while. That makes some kind of sense if you're considered a major writer in modern American literature. But my stories belong to the horror genre, which is by definition in the realm of pop culture.

I mentioned previously that "The Frolic" was written under peculiar circumstances. I explain what these are in an essay I wrote for the book that's packaged with the DVD of the film—the short film, to be accurate, since its running time is only about twenty-four minutes. Simply put, at that early point in my efforts to become a horror writer, I was hungry to get published—not an unnatural desire—and it seemed to me at the time that the best way to get published was to write a horror story that featured normal characters who come to be the victims of a menacing supernatural force or being, which is the template for the great majority of horror stories. I wanted the reader to be able to imagine that the husband and wife who are the protagonists of the story could jump in their car with their daughter Norleen and drive off to Disney World. This has to do with my point about the atmosphere of Poe's stories deriving in a significant way from their removal from the everyday, waking world so that they could get to that place of mystery from where our impulses and conceptions, everything on which our surface sense of reality rests. I think the fact that "The Frolic" had such a footing in the normal world is what made it adaptable as a film, or at least a short film.

What got pushed into the background, though, was the abnormal, mysterious world of the supernatural, child-killing psycho of the story, John Doe. What movies do is show things, and there are just some things that can't be shown without trivializing them, demystifying them, or making them appear just plain silly. Fortunately, this missing piece from the story was more than adequately compensated for by the actor Maury Sterling, who really brought to life the character of John Doe. In the story "The Frolic," John Doe is someone who is only developed in a second-hand way through the account of another party. In the film, he's right there in front of you and plays a larger role in the narrative. It made "The Frolic" real for me in a way it hadn't been before.

As for the comic books, I got a kick out of the fact that those who seemed to be their main consumers had never heard of me. That's not usually the case as far as I know.

Are you fascinated by blackness, or is it merely a truer form of the crumminess of existence? To me, crumminess and decay are actually attractive, seductive qualities. They're picturesque in some aesthetically demented way. A sort of hypnotic enchantment attaches to them. To my sensibility, they don't feel like stages on the way to blackness. One can lose oneself in places and conditions of crumminess and decay. They're a refuge in which self-annihilation can take place without the terrors of death. It's definitely a perverse proclivity, a sinking into total decadence. The French have an expression, nostalgie de la boue, which literally translates as "nostalgia for the mud." It can have different meanings depending on the context, but in the sense I'm using this phrase it means a desire to regress to a lower state of being or to proceed into degeneration, corruption, wallowing in the sordid and the soiled.

There's nothing crummy about blackness, and blackness is not something wherein decay can obtain. To tell you the truth, I didn't realize the obsession I had with blackness until Brian Stableford pointed it out in the entry he wrote on my stories in the reference book *Horror, Ghost, and Gothic Writers*. I remember being impressed decades ago by Edmund Burke's discussion of blackness, darkness, and obscurity in his aesthetic treatise *On the Sublime and the Beautiful*, but I wouldn't count that as a direct influence on my own use of blackness in my horror stories. As a symbol, a concept, and a condition, blackness is the end of the road, and that's where I've usually tried to take each of my stories. At some point I came up with a strategy for developing a narrative that I thought of as "upping the ante." The idea was to keep pushing the horror element in a story as far as I could before I felt I couldn't push it any farther without its devolving into incoherency. I'm sure that some of those who have read my stuff have felt that too often I've pushed too far.

To me it seems obvious that Lovecraft did much the same thing, both in his plots and in his prose style. His stories are loaded with passages in which you can really feel him straining as hard as he can toward some

> "Poe's stories don't focus on supernatural elements. But they do take place in a world that is evil, desolate, and suffused with a profound sense of doom."

absolute expression of mad horror. A lot of critics find such passages to be damning of his ability as a prose writer, but they are in fact what define his work and give it the force that it has. Poe did much the same, and this has caused certain critics of "taste" to relegate his work to a lower order of literature. There is definitely a strong element of vulgarity in the histrionic prose of both Poe and Lovecraft. In my view, vulgarity is an inherent quality of great horror literature. The only issue is a writer's aptitude in using vulgarity to reach a level of effect that's not achievable in any other way.

Some supernatural writers exhibit no vulgarity at all in their writing. Among these writers are Walter de la Mare, Robert Aickman, Vernon Lee, Edith Wharton, and Oliver Onions. The works of these writers definitely have their charm, but it resides in a quality that's the opposite of vulgarity. That quality is urbanity, which just doesn't make for horror fiction that gets under the skin of readers and clings to their consciousness. Both Poe and Lovecraft advocated suggestiveness and mystery in horror fiction, but for the things they wanted to express they also needed vulgarity. The other writers I've named here had entirely different aims in their work. In my view, they didn't feel the deep disturbance about existence that Poe and Lovecraft did. They were horror writers of manners rather than madness. ℮

*For more information:
www.ligotti.net

Weiroot

BY JEFFREY FORD

ILLUSTRATION BY GRANDE OMBRE

IN WHICH AN
ALIEN BABY IS
NOT QUITE AS
STRANGE AS ITS
NEW FATHER

EIROOT, YOU MAD MAN, what do you think you're doing, sitting in the chill of the night, winking at the winking stars? Are you sending them a message? Come visit me? And what if they were to? What if in say a year or two a star fell, swept down out of the dark, trailing green fire, and smashed with an explosion of sparks and black diamond debris into the dunes surrounding your wooden plank palace? What would you do then? Oh sure, you'd call for your four marble men without faces, those savage quadruplets whose stone sculpted arms move with supple grace. "If they get obstreperous, let them have it," you'd whisper and the four white dolts would nod and flex. But then, imagine your surprise, when the rock from space breaks open and out crawls a little fat baby, purple as a plum with a ridge of webbed spikes like a ladies open fan running from the crown of its head back to the base of the skull, orange eyes and a little "o" of a mouth. You know you'd gasp and wave your arms in the air...well; at least you'd wear a

look of consternation and shake your head, and who wouldn't? But then, even the four stone flunkies would make amazed faceless expressions when the little fellow from beyond the moon says "Feed me, Weiroot," in a psychic voice that sounds between the ears. That would snarl your line of thought. So, I can see it now, you'd scoop that star baby up in your robed arms and shuffle with your lame stride back into that cockeyed palace. Then what? A cold leg of mutton? A rasher of game hens from the forest beyond the dunes? Octopus and eel heads you purchased that morning from Yakus, The Bold But Battered? And the miracle is the babe devours all of it. That's right, that cute little mouth holds rows of needle teeth, and he's got an appetite. He takes off one of the stone goons' index fingers in the feeding. Then surprise and a portion of horror when the mewling fright drops a neat little pile of space scat onto the clean swept floor of the dining room. You'd be screaming orders like a second lieutenant in the pontiff's royal guard, "Drop the rose petals!" "Man the shovel! Haste and earnest effort in the name of all that's holy!" And after the tumult and chaos of the exigencies of biologic existence, then the quiet time, holding the snoozing fin-head cradled in your arms, rocking in the rocker next to your telescope out on the open air observatory while the wind transforms the face of the dunes to a whole new physiognomy, the ocean laps the shore in the distance to the south, and the night birds sing in the forest. In that peaceful time, that's when the deal will be sealed and you'll promise your life in protection and care for the helpless fellow. Because, Weiroot, even though your face is a rippling moonscape of healed wounds, your posture is worse than that of your listing home, and you're feared by those who don't know you as a strange and cantankerous entity outside of society, The Man Who Escaped Hell, you are no more nor less than any man—a hungry heart and a wavering will. That's right, don't deny it. You're thinking, "Here's my family. Here's my opportu-

nity to care and have someone return the emotion." I see right through your schemes. Your thoughts are utterly transparent to me. And oh, what great pleasure you will derive from naming the wee beast, like it's a puppy, like it's your own invention. You'll try Hartvill, Tharnweb, Wenslav, to see how they roll off the tongue, every now and then checking the child's countenance to see if the word fits the face like a tailored mask. But all along, all along, you know you're slowly but resolutely spiraling in a decreasing orbit toward Weiroot Junior or Weiroot II, and the excitement of that has your big toe itching in your eel skin ankle boot. When you're just about to grasp for one of these narcissistic monikers, something grabs you instead, some dim glimmer of reason, and you veer off and christen the child Oondeshai, which was the name of an island in Hell. Then a kiss to that purple brow and you lean back in your rocker and rock beneath the stars from whence he came, closing your eyes and falling into a dream of the future. Beautiful. Or so you think, but wait, Weiroot. Just a second. Dreams are dreams and the future is like a hall of mirrors reflecting the past and offering up wavering illusions until everything shatters and you're cut to ribbons by shards of reality. Allow me to suggest where all this is leading. Little Oondeshai will be both a pleasure and a trial for some time, and, though difficult at first, you'll learn to give of yourself, to feed, comfort, and care for your charge. Your stone men will be put through their paces as they'd never been, even in the ancient time when they were created to serve and protect Satan, long before you found them in the cave in the sea cliff and brought them to life with an inadvertent sneeze. There will rise up a hurricane of activity in the wooden palace, all centered on the child, and every action will embrace him as its eye. This won't necessarily be bad, for it will take you away from your melancholic study, it will resurrect you from your pointless pondering of the stars. I don't deny there will be long walks among the dunes in which you will tell the boy stories, half true, half the product of your own skittering imagination, like the one about the man who teaches the monkey to be a man while the monkey teaches the man to be a monkey and they switch places only to discover deep philosophical truths they'd never before conceived of until the man puts the monkey in a cage and the monkey escapes and kills the man and then is shot by the man's wife, who loved the monkey turned man more than the man turned monkey. Yes, you'll fill the child's head with that kind of simplistic clap trap to make him a dreamer, and he'll show no revulsion when he runs his fingertips over your scarred, tree bark face. Together you'll fly dragon kites, running over the dunes, in the slanting light of cool evenings. You'll fish for Tillibar skeeners off the ocean cliffs with a long rope, a hook to snag Leviathan, and the stone quadruplets heaving and ho-ing, hoisting the wriggling silver behemoths of the deep high up the cliffside in the full moonlight. You'll teach him something like right from wrong, and punish him by confining him to his room. He'll stamp and howl like a fox in a leg trap and pass through the walls a hundred times, for this will be one of his special powers, and you'll patiently catch him and put him back and tell him NO! He'll, of course, say, "I hate you Weiroot, you turd." You'll know he doesn't mean it, but still, these words will prick your heart like a thistle in the thumb. Later, there'll be the reconciliation and you'll give him an orange sugar god on a stick for apologizing. Time will change you both like the wind changes the dunes. Both of you will grow, he physically, you inwardly, expanding to care for two. His purple complexion will lighten to a pale violet. His fin will recede to become a mere ridge of lumps. He'll lose the webbing on his fingers and toes, the split in his tongue will meld to a single point. He'll grow taller than you, and his alien abilities will manifest themselves—his ability to detect a lie, to see in the dark, to speak to the dead and know the secret thoughts of the marble quadruplets. All of this will have a profound effect upon you. Just to know that your stone servants have had inner-lives, dreams and anguish, all along will weigh upon your conscience, and you'll finally be forced to give them their freedom and bid them well in the world. They'll leave you one day at the end of summer when the leaves in the forest have begun to change and each will choose a direction of the compass and strike out on his own. You'll extend them each the favor of a pouch of coins, a knife, and a painted expression you or Oondeshai will draw upon their blank faces with the indelible ink of the red octopus. A smile for one, a frown for another, a quizzical look for his brother, and the last will be marked to show compassion. Then they'll be gone and it will be you and Oondeshai. And he'll ask you about your past, and there will be no way to lie to him. So you'll have to say, "I'm the man who escaped from Hell." But this answer will only give birth to a hundred more questions and you'll walk with him on a bright morning over the dunes to the edge of the ocean and there you'll sit as the waves lap your feet and you'll tell him everything. "I, Weiroot, committed an unpardonable sin," you'll say. "Why?" he'll ask. And you'll begin, hemming and hawing at first, and then your confession will flow like blood.

Jeffrey Ford is the author of The Well-Built City Trilogy—*The Physiognomy, Memoranda, The Beyond* (from Golden Gryphon)—and the novels *The Portrait of Mrs. Charbuque*, *The Girl in the Glass*, and *The Shadow Year* (from Harper Collins). His short stories have been collected in three volumes: *The Fantasy Writer's Assistant*, *The Empire of Ice Cream*, and *The Drowned Life*. He lives in South Jersey and teaches literature and writing at Brookdale Community College.

The Garbacologist

BY JEFF JOHNSON

ILLUSTRATION BY FOX

IN WHICH AN
APPETITE IS
NOT SO MUCH
GOURMET AS IT
IS GROTESQUE

STARING AT THE rows of glass bottles across the bar, Turner wondered about the skeleton of his childhood cat. It had likely spread into the water table of the city and become part of the teeth of children who would grow to tell lies. The misshapen blue marbles of lost hope and the tokens of broken dreams that fell from the hair of those around them would roll into cracks and corners and gather dust until the garbacologist picked them up, or they were eaten.

Turner tossed back a tumbler of sweet well bourbon and his eyes drifted across the mirrored backsplash to the burned out neon sign in the window behind him. It was getting dark outside. Dreams and lost hopes would fill the gutters shortly, and some of them might have worth.

He clicked open a dented cigarette case and selected Leon Sun's chrome knuckle bone from the odd assortment of sculptures inside. The low shock of holding it between his naked fingertips was no preparation for the higher resonance of dropping it into his mouth. His flared nostrils flooded with ozone.

Turner's face lit into a beatific smile of barely controlled violence and he raised two fingers for a double. He rolled the knuckle bone between molars and cheek, to clear his tongue in case he felt like bitching someone out. His shoulders relaxed and a graceful fluidity crept up his spine. The old door chime rang behind him. Turner leered at the reflection of the huge shape that blocked the doorway.

"You're a hard man to find. I've been looking for you for two days." Fullman settled onto the bar stool next to him, panting. Fat didn't describe Fullman. He was round, forced into an old but well cared for tweed suit, the kind of Savile Row affair that got better with age. He smelled like talcum powder and wet rust. The old nails in the bar groaned as Fullman leaned on it.

"Is that right?" Turner faced Fullman and his eyes narrowed to slits. "What the fuck you want, fat man?"

"To tell you a story," Fullman replied. The expression painted on his spherical face was one of innocence, but there was a steady tic in the egg-sized pouch under his right eye.

"I'm busy, Fullman. Go peddle it somewhere else." Turner tossed a ten dollar bill onto the bar and slid off his stool.

"Leon's knuckle bone, eh?" Fullman's smile turned mocking. "But it won't make you brave enough to swallow it, hmm?"

It was the same old argument. He left Fullman sitting where he was. As he opened the door on the wet night Fullman called out.

"Your little rabbits all faced west two days ago, didn't they?" Turner froze in the doorway. "I know why. Find me after you take that thing out of your mouth and you're smart enough to be scared."

Turner stepped outside and let the door close behind him.

HE TROLLED THE alleys on the east side regularly, which is probably how Fullman had found him. But he never walked in this part of town without Leon Sun's relic in his head. It was too dangerous.

Two glassy-eyed street thugs with gold teeth, big jackets and stocking caps studied him as he turned into the mouth of the alley behind the bar. One of them reached up and withdrew the toothpick from his mouth.

Turner's head snapped in their direction. They paused at the look on his face, smiles half-formed.

"Put that pick back in your mouth. Now."

The guy shrugged and turned away, his hand moving slowly back to his mouth. Turner brushed past them, clipping one of them with his shoulder. He heard a nervous giggle somewhere off to his left.

It was in this set of alleys that he had found Leon's chrome knuckle, and many of the other articles in his cigarette case. Small groups loitered around, waiting for something to happen. Young women strutted around on business. Small lines formed here and there, creating an aura of low grade commerce.

She was somewhere between sixteen and dead, tucked between two trash cans, her tiny hooker's purse open in the lap of her plastic mini skirt, a bent spoon sticking out the top. Turner knelt next to her and studied her slack face. He'd never seen her before.

She was nodding, high after her first score of the night. His pulse quickened as he pawed through the debris around her. He found it next to her left hand, a tiny silver tooth with a flute of bright metal curling off it. He picked it up and examined it, then raised it to his lips and blew. A sad, lofty, slightly off note rang down the brick corridor. She gave up singing because she wasn't very good. No one took her dream from her. She just gave it away. Turner dropped the small object into her open purse and wiped his hand on his pants. In a city this size tooth flutes were unremarkable.

Everybody lost something. Most of them never noticed until it was long gone. Some never did notice. To a garbacologist with the

right kind of eye, the lost items were everywhere.

Turner thought about this for the first time in years as he wandered the streets and alleys, looking for something interesting. Leon brooded in his eyes and lent a predatory dance to his steps, ensuring that he was alone with his thoughts.

Fullman was right. Something had disrupted the stratum of garbage in the last two days. There was less of it, for one thing. It had started when he'd noticed the suicide bunnies all facing west.

Give up singing and a tooth flute might fall unnoticed from your sleeve. Sicken of violent crime and you might lose an eleventh knuckle bone made of metal. Horseshoes were everywhere, as were bicycle wheels and things half paintbrush/half crayon, but they were nothing compared to the stone pennies around ATM machines or the glass tears on the steps of every church. And all paled in number to the little blue marbles that rained from children's hair. Kill yourself, and a suicide bunny will hop out of the box where your personal belongings were thoughtfully condensed.

The bunnies ate every token of human transformation they could. There was a certain logic there, a cold spiral Turner recognized but rarely thought about. Some of the tokens, like the ones in his cigarette case, were surpassingly beautiful or exceedingly odd. Fullman coveted Turner's collection of rarities with an appetite that was an unsavory parody of the diligent suicide bunnies. The fat man would have swallowed this evening's bland tooth flute like a walrus sucking down a generic anchovy.

Turner emerged from an alley onto a wide boulevard. The gutters, normally lined with blue marbles, were empty. No shining object caught his eye for as far as he could see in either direction. A lone bunny stood like a sentry at the edge of a pool of light three street lamps away.

Fullman called the bunnies trenchermen and perceived them as chicken-shaped brass boilers with gates in their faces and black iron spades for wings. He wondered briefly what that said about Fullman's psychology, or what it said about his own for that matter. Turner saw them as stuffed rabbits, with large, blank, mismatched eyes made of poorly stitched black cloth. They sat permanently upright on flat feet and had no arms. The cloth of their bodies was a dull russet and gave off the kind of flickering light you might see through your closed eyelids when your face was pointed at a TV in an otherwise dark room. They moved slowly, hopping once every hour or so, sometimes not for days, as though they were forever winding down no matter how much they ate. He had never watched them feed as he knew Fullman had.

And now something was cleaning the streets and the suicide bunnies were behaving oddly. Turner hailed a cab and as soon as he was in back he spit Leon's knucklebone into a rag from his pocket and dropped it back into the case.

The emptiness of the streets immediately filled him with dread. Either people had quit thinking or something new had come to town.

"You ever get tired of driving a cab?" Turner asked. It was always nice to have Leon back in his box.

"Job is job." The driver glanced into the rearview mirror, a pair of small Sri Lankan eyes under tousled hair. "Why, you wanna drive cab?"

"Don't think I'd like it," Turner replied. "All this geometry. Too much like a cemetery, man."

"What you mean?" The driver turned down the soft chatter of the radio dispatcher.

"Just that there's something missing. Look out there." Turner's eyes wandered over the bland, dark cityscape. He had never seen it so clean, and that made everything worse. "I sometimes think we've crossed a line. People started painting in caves, and gradually the making and building got more

complicated, until we got to palaces and churches. Ever see those old buildings in Europe with the gargoyles on them?"

"Same in Sri Lanka, but they tear down and make new. Bigger, not so pretty, but elevators work."

"Then you can see my point. Form vs function. What a terrible concept, to put the two in opposition. We've lost the impulse to put soul into things."

The driver shrugged.

"Think about it," Turner continued. "You drive these grids all night, memorizing numbers and the size and shape of inert, meaningless landmarks. Its like sitting in a dark room and chanting zero. You ever wonder what that's doing to you?"

"It do nothing," the driver replied. He glanced into the rearview again, his eyes narrowed.

"Exactly," Turner replied. The driver turned on to east 28th, a wide boulevard lined with symmetry. Turner closed his eyes, suddenly tired. He leaned against the door. The window was cold against his cheek and smelled like hair gel.

"So what you do?" the driver chirped. "You sell weed, eh?"

"I dig through trash," Turner replied. "It's the only place where a modern city is an old church."

It was this very sentiment that had led him to garbacology in the first place. Looking deeper into the world around him he had eventually turned to trash, the most telling way to peek up the urban skirt. Unlike a criminal or industrial garbacologist, Turner had gone after it with a verve borne of philosophy.

In the first few years he had struggled, until he refined the practice and learned where to look. The supers of various buildings would call him at certain times. He made contacts with cleaning agencies and movers. It wasn't long before he had built up a steady trade of old records, vintage clothes, books, and even some decent antiques. People were throwing away or leaving behind a rich, dusty, sometimes moist cornucopia, and he mined it all.

It was a shot glass in a gaudy collection that first caught his eye. There was something special about one of them, but he couldn't tell why. The collection itself was amateurish, and the glass itself was from Vegas. He kept it on a whim. Later he drank from it, and knew with a strange certainty that it was the glass the collector had sipped his last drink from.

After that he had looked more closely at things, and the closer he looked, the more he found.

The cab driver cursed and leaned on the horn. Turner jerked upright. They had arrived at his hotel, a shabby little place he'd moved into three weeks ago, following his pattern of moving every month.

"God damn UPS." The driver rolled down the window. "Move that fucking truck!"

Turner's mouth slammed shut. The cigarette case in his pocket pinged and vibrated like it was full of live roaches.

The truck was huge, its wheels as high as a man. The twin tines of its forward dumpster lifters had shovels on the ends. The entire pitted steel surface was unpainted and gave off the sickly russet luminosity of the bunnies. It was facing them, idling in the mouth of the hotel parking lot next to the winking vacancy sign. A dim red light glowed in the interior of the cab, silhouetting a figure inside. The enormous engine revved once, vomiting black diesel smoke from twin upright exhaust columns. The cigarette case in Turner's pocket chattered like a set of wind-up teeth.

"What that truck doing out so late?" the driver wondered aloud. It was three AM.

"It must be stolen," Turner whispered hoarsely. The driver's description of it as a UPS truck rather than the hellish thing Turner saw sent a wild shock of pure terror through him. "Back us away and floor it."

The silhouette's head slowly turned back and forth, saying no.

The cab driver peeled out in reverse and then nearly gutted the transmission as he slammed it into drive. As they raced past the dump truck its headlights swirled and dimmed to burnt orange.

"Left!" Turner cried, looking back. The dump truck rolled out after them, its arms lowering. Angry plumes of sparks showered down its sides as the shovels touched the pavement. The shriek of metal on asphalt was deafening.

The driver slewed right and made a quick succession of turns, cursing steadily in his own language. The dump truck slowed and eventually disappeared behind. The chattering of the objects in his cigarette case quieted.

Turner knew the truck could have overtaken them, but for some reason had let them go. He took a deep breath and wiped the sweat from his forehead with the back of his sleeve. His heart was racing so he turned his eyes away from the awful, portentous emptiness of the quiet streets. His mind played a tired trick, filling the darkness with the ghostly weave of a chain link fence.

They pulled into a taxi substation, a barn of a building filled with exhaust and the hum of air compressors and pneumatic drills. The bright halogen lights hurt his eyes. The driver pulled into an empty space and cut the engine, then turned around. Turner noticed that he was old.

"So you dig through trash, eh?" His eyes were hard and flat. He hadn't enjoyed being chased by a stolen UPS truck. Turner nodded.

"Maybe what you find not so good. Maybe you leave alone. Sometimes people throw away things not because they broke or old. Maybe they can't stand to have." He watched Turner's face for a reaction.

"What's the damage," Turner asked. The driver shook his head.

"No charge for you. Your money dirty, trash man. I pick up one man, I look back, I see another. Different eyes. Thief in a truck

chase my cab. I get bad feeling from you. You keep money. I never that poor."

He got out of the driver seat and slammed the door. Turner leaned forward and peered over the divider. There was a token on the seat, a tiny compass without symbols. He hoped it had been there for a while, and was not from tonight. He shouldn't have talked to the old man. It was a bad night all around.

Turner got out and walked past a row of brightly lit vending machines, through the jumble of cabs with their hoods up and out into the night. There was a line of pay phones outside the building. He found one that worked and then dug through his wallet for a card he'd hoped to never use.

E. A. Fullman, Gourmand and Purveyor of Fine Curios. Turner tried all three of the numbers and got no answer. On impulse he called his hotel and dialed the code for his room. He had three new messages. The first one was from Fullman. He sounded out of breath.

"Turner, its Fullman. Time appears to be shorter than I'd hoped. I've called a meeting of the Society of Garbacologists. I don't know why I'm calling you as you've always declined membership, but if you're looking for answers meet us at the restaurant where we first approached you. They have agreed to stay open until this matter is resolved." The recording said the message had been left just past midnight, three hours ago.

The second message began with a long stretch of silence broken only with the distant static of the line, then came three deep, hollow booms, the sound of a heavy hand knocking on a door.

The last message was a solid minute of the high pitched scream of a metal saw cutting through something solid. Turner waited all the way through it and then hung up the phone.

The bistro in question was only a few minutes away. He hailed the first cab that left the substation and rode silently after

giving the sleepy driver the address. The dark streets along the way were bare of blue marbles and artifacts, as though an army of street sweepers had scoured the city.

The red curtains were drawn closed when they arrived. Turner paid and approached the door. He looked both ways before opening it. A tiny bell rang.

A waiter led him across the polished hardwood floor to Fullman's table. It was the largest in the room, set with fifteen places, one for every member of Fullman's garbacology society. All of the chairs were empty except for Fullman's two-seat arrangement at the head of the table.

Every inch of the white linen surface was covered with carefully plated confections, all cold and untouched, the fats congealed and the sauces broken. A bottle of white wine rested beside the enormous man, three quarters empty.

Fullman looked up from his study of the untouched banquet, his round head rising like it weighed a thousand pounds. His normally rosy cheeks were pale as wax lilies and his beady, porcine eyes were moist in their sockets and slow to focus.

"Turner," he rumbled eventually, as though he'd run into him in a cave in Chile. "I can't believe you made it… You of all people."

"I almost didn't." Turner pulled out a chair and sat down.

"I know." Fullman sloshed more wine into his glass and drained it, his catcher's mitt of a throat barely moving. "We're all that's left, just the two of us."

Turner crossed his arms. "A truck was waiting for me tonight. Is that what came to town two days ago, when the suicide bunnies all turned west?"

For once Fullman didn't sneer at the distinction between trenchermen and bunnies. He soberly swirled the inch of wine left in his glass.

"Some years ago a wandering garbacologist came to town. I met him in the lobby of the Catholic Hospital of all places, so there

was enough for both of us. I was gorging myself on dreams of another tomorrow, failed youth, all the things we could have done." He waved one hand as he talked, making a little song of it, then sighed.

"He was from up north, some industrial city, I forget which one. It was thick, he said. They waded through rivers of blue pearls and lost wheels, things we never dreamt of here. And then one day, one street at a time, it all disappeared." Fullman looked up, his eyes wider than Turner would have thought possible.

"Something was cleaning up, taking the garbage away. Not eating it, not hiding it, but moving it en masse!"

"I don't get it," Turner said. "Who is it? And moving it where? Why?"

"I don't know. I am so full, Turner, but I cannot rush a process that takes forever. The fatter I get the more I want. Whatever it is, it's a bigger fish than I am, older and fatter by some order of magnitude. Last night there was some speculation that it might represent the pinnacle of our food chain."

"You mean a trash man."

Fullman jerked as though he'd been slapped. His fat face rippled and distorted.

"I beg your pardon!" he thundered. Spit blew from his purple lips. Turner could see tiny gray teeth behind them.

"Something a cab driver mistakenly called me earlier. The trash man. No amount of bunnies or trenchermen can clean it all up, even with your help. It's like biology, Fullman, or economics."

Fullman gradually regained his composure, his head bowed. When he looked up there was a slyness about his eyes, his rosebud mouth puckered primly.

"Remember when we first met? It was at the train station as I recall. I saw you stoop to pick up the lead match stick that fell from that arsonist's pant leg. Is it still warm?" Fullman furtively licked his lips.

"It is." Turner kept it in the cigarette case. Each time he put it into his mouth the severe, brutal buildings of the city made some temporary sense. Like all arsonists, the man in the train station had pretensions of architecture.

"Ahh, good. As I remember, I approached you and we talked as you looked around. It took you a few minutes to realize that we saw the same thing."

"We don't see the same thing, Fullman. Not really. I see things I want to keep, to save from oblivion. You see things you want to eat."

Fullman waved his hand dismissively. "Semantics."

"Remember the maggots? The ones in the cream pastry by the tracks? That really made you mad, didn't it."

"You mockingly called the maggots 'disco rice', Turner, and now you rudely beat me to the point of my story. I knew then that we were destined to hate each other, and now I sincerely and truly despise you. You hail from a low place."

Turner found himself smiling. Fullman snorted in disgust.

"You're like some vulgar, sooty little bird, flitting from one hotel to the next, collecting your bright little trinkets, too afraid of your shadow to swallow anything. You lack the regal waist of a refined garbacologist. I and the members of my society grew bloated with hopes and dreams, and we might have dined until our skins stretched to cover the world. I don't know why I've gone out of my way to save a misguided runt such as yourself, except perhaps for some final company."

He produced a folded handkerchief from his vest pocket and leaned forward. His swollen fingers moved with tremendous delicacy as he unwrapped it.

"Look," he whispered, holding it out. "Its one of my childhood dreams, the only one I could locate on such short notice."

Turner leaned forward. In the center of the handkerchief was a chef's hat made of pristine white cloth, starched and standing up so that it resembled a button mushroom.

"You wanted to be a cook?"

"Evidently at one time I did. Or a baker, they wear these too. I can't remember. Apparently someone convinced me it was impossible, or I convinced myself. I have a feeling I did it when I learned with someone better. But of course," he said, eyeing the hat on his palm, "with some token regret."

"You're going to eat that?"

"I am." Fullman's voice was a cracked rumble almost too low to make out. "It's that or the rendering truck. To eat your child-

hood dream or your own lost hope is to change your essence, your very nature. The man that sits before you will leave this room with a new set of aspirations. I will not know your face, Turner, and that is my sole consolation. I will be safe; to live whatever life I can inside of this broken, unsuitable delusion."

He raised the tiny hat and inverted it like a thimble between the sausages of his fingers. Tears dribbled down his cheeks in two oily streams. "To you, Turner. You were an unworthy adversary at best, and a sorely lacking companion at this crucial time. I consider you a bad omen."

He folded the tiny hat into his cavernous mouth and raised the last of the wine to his trembling lips, his face spasming. His mouth worked and his eyes went wide as the hat traveled down his esophagus. His enormous bulk forcefully contracted.

Totems and artifacts rained from his sparse crop of rat-brown hair. Bright objects fountained from his tweed sleeves and clattered to the polished floor. A steady racket sounded around his ankles. Fullman's groan rose to a howl and he arched back, explosively deflating like a punctured balloon.

Turner rose and backed away. The steady beep of a large vehicle in reverse was parallaxing closer. The floor vibrated, and a whiff of diesel exhaust mingled with Fullman's cold feast.

Turner sprinted across the empty floor and slammed through a set of swinging doors into the kitchen, startling the waiter who sat slumped over a magazine. Turner held up a finger for silence, flicked open his cigarette case and tossed Leon Sun's knuckle bone into his mouth. His sinuses burning with ozone, he glared at the waiter. A bell rang as the front door of the bistro swung open.

"Don't go out there," Turner growled. "Show me the back door."

The waiter raised an unsteady arm and pointed. Turner ran.

IT WAS JUST before sunrise when the cab dropped him off in a residential area some distance to the west. Turner paid and watched the cab's lights turn the corner and disappear, then he slowly walked into the yellow pool under the nearest street light. There he opened his cigarette case and examined the contents one last time.

They were all special, made more so by the time he'd spent carrying them around, keeping them safe. He brought the box closer to his face as though to smell them.

The noble copper thumbtack of a great teacher brought low by illness rested next to the arsonist's lead match, forever warm. Savage Leon's chrome knuckle, a tiny test tube containing a single perfect kernel of corn, the pumpkin colored owl, an obsidian .22 caliber bullet engraved with pine cones, a tiny spider silk umbrella, and the precious ear-shaped broken prayer lost in the streets outside a doctor's office by a mother holding the hand of her mute son, all stories written in a language he'd never know again. Silently, he emptied the box into the grass at his feet and turned to the house that had been his childhood home.

It looked smaller, of course. None of the lights were on. There was a newish car parked in the driveway. He walked across the street and up the drive, then along the side of the house into the back yard. There was no need to go into the house, and it would have been impractical without Leon. There was one lost hope in the back yard.

The fig tree stood like a black hand against the pre-dawn sky, grown huge as the house had not. Its branches started about head height and were thick with the fruit that he knew would yield a sticky white sap he had once confused with glue. He reached up and began to climb.

Turner assumed that the blue marble that had no doubt popped from his head when his mother let his cat die in the garage had been eaten by a suicide bunny long ago, but while he couldn't guess what form it had taken, he knew something had been lost in the higher branches, out of their reach, and thankfully the tree had grown wide enough to support his full weight.

It was wedged in the vee of the trunk, his token, a tiny cube, the symbol of permanence. Turner pulled it from the bark and put it in his mouth, remembering.

They were moving, and he was looking at a decade of what seemed then and shaped up to be an unsettling period of sofas, basements, and relatives who wanted no part of him. There had been a girl named Ann, with long blond hair and faded blue eyes. Her alcoholic mother, always dressed in a tattered pink robe, had made canned chili for them when he had shared the grim news. The next day Ann had shown up on her bike after school as always and pretended nothing was going to happen, even though everything was in boxes on the driveway and they were leaving in the morning. She kissed him in this fig tree, and a type of hope, a figment of whatever a child finds safety in, had tumbled from his hair and come to rest where he'd found it, locked in a lusterless cube he had to swallow.

He took it out of his mouth and stared at it, letting it fade to the dim spark that flowed through his fingers. He had lost it so long ago that his personality had been shaped without it, his final form growing around and through its absence.

Glistening in the bark next to his hand was a small silver ring, Ann's no doubt. He reached for it and then slowly pulled his hand back. The time for his handling of such objects had passed.

The high trill of air brakes shattered the stillness, followed by the low rumble of a distant, massive engine. Tendrils of diesel exhaust curled through the branches of the fig tree. Turner put the cube back in his mouth, took a deep breath through his nose and swallowed. The little silver ring by his hand grew dim and faded to nothing.

Turner gazed up through the branches at the gray dawn sky, realizing that something had happened to him but not knowing what it was. He knew he didn't live anywhere in particular and had no real job, and for the first time this seemed of burning importance. He was also high in a fig tree on a gray dawn, in the yard of a small house he had not seen in years.

He climbed out of the tree and walked to the street on shaky legs. The neighborhood showed signs of waking. Light spilled from a scattering of windows and a UPS truck idled in front of the house across the street. Turner waved uncertainly. The truck ground through its gears and drove away. He watched it go with a blank expression that mirrored what he felt.

The morning dew had settled into his clothes. Turner put his hands in his pockets and started walking with his head down, confused and exhausted and feeling somehow light, or hollow. He never noticed the little twist of old foil that fell from his pant leg. It might have been a thimble, or a miniature garbage can.

A block to the south, a suicide bunny turned north and hopped. ☉

Jeff Johnson is an artist and writer living in Portland, Oregon. He's been tattooing professionally for nearly two decades and is the managing co-owner of the Sea Tramp Tattoo Company. His memoir *Tattoo Machine* will be available in hardcover this summer. Be sure to visit your local bookseller or go to Amazon.com.

Headstone In Your Pocket

BY PAUL TREMBLAY

ILLUSTRATION BY STEVEN ARCHER

IN WHICH THE

PAST IS NEITHER

SUFFICIENTLY

DEAD NOR

FULLY BURIED

The sun is high but it feels low, its heat close and heavy enough to push heads down and slump shoulders. Border Patrol Agent Joe Marquez runs his hand along the tractor-trailer and chips of white paint break off and crumble to dust under his fingertips like dried leaves from a dead houseplant. There are rustling noises inside the truck, trapped spirits, humanity in a tin can. He wonders if they'll emerge in any better shape than the trailer's paint job.

Two agents pin the driver against the truck's chrome grille. He yells, claiming the hot chrome burns his skin. The agents don't care, don't say anything, and handcuff him. The smuggler is priority one. The cargo can wait.

Joe jogs the length of the trailer and yells ahead, "Let's go, get those doors open, now!"

Local commuters and smugglers and immigrants know the Tubac checkpoint's schedule. The checkpoint is thirty miles south of Tucson and thirty miles north of Nogales and the Mexico-U.S. border. It was supposed to be closed at this mid-afternoon hour, but the Border Patrol office in Tucson, which prominently features a photo of John Wayne (circa *The Alamo*) on its wall, received an anonymous tip, a tip that turned out to be true.

One agent turns the rusted handle and throws open the trailer's doors while another agent aims his automatic rifle. Heat, sweat, and a low, desperate collected conversation rush out of the trailer and into the surrounding desert. There is no air conditioning and the temperature inside is over one hundred and ten degrees. Flashlights penetrate the darkness and reveal a mass of bodies, scores of men picking up their heads but hiding their eyes, holding out empty hands.

They'll be unarmed, they will not hurt anyone, and they'll have nothing on them. All will be processed for deportation. Joe has been a Border Patrol Agent for two years and has witnessed the same sorry scene at least twice a month.

The Tubac checkpoint is a temporary one, with its portable lights and generators resting on the shoulder of I-19, alongside its incendiary local politics. The suburbanites don't want a fixed checkpoint because checkpoint towns become a de-facto second border, fearing smugglers and immigrants and other dangerous (non-white) criminals would use their sleepy little towns as way stations, drug factories, and shoot 'em ups. The Border Patrol's Tucson sector comprises almost the entire Arizona-Mexico border and is the only sector without at least one fixed checkpoint.

Agents separate the fifty men into groups of ten. The men are a task to be divvied up. They are sweaty, exhausted, and frightened, but everyone makes it out of the trailer alive and conscious. Joe's ten stands in a line and with their hands held out and open although he did not tell them to do so. Joe pats them down. The third in line has something in the front left pocket of his jeans. Joe says, "¿Cuál es su nombre?" being rigidly formal in the request, an attempt to give a measure of respect and dignity, but he knows it could very well be interpreted as one of la migra flaunting his position.

The man says, "Guillermo." He's tall, and skinny, a piece of string hanging from the leg of his cut-off jean shorts. Guillermo has thick beard stubble overwriting a map of acne scars and he is likely a full decade older than Joe is, but there's no way to tell. He doesn't have a passport.

Joe says, "Guillermo, dame lo que tienes un tu bolsillo. Por favor."

"No es nada. No son drogas." *It is nothing. It is not drugs.* His speech pattern is as formal as Joe's. The two men are actors afraid of forgetting their lines. He reaches into his pocket and gives Joe what he wants. It's a folded rectangle of tinfoil.

"Entonces, ¿qué es?"

"Es de m'hijo."

Joe unwraps the tinfoil slowly. It sits open on his palm, a metal flower with petals dancing in the warm breeze. In the middle, there's a small, clear plastic baggie, and inside the baggie is a white rock. Joe takes it out and realizes it is a tooth, a baby tooth, small as a pebble, so inconsequential and fragile that it might blow away in the scalding desert winds, or simply disintegrate.

THE LIGHTS ARE dim. Local country songs alternate with Johnny Cash standards on the jukebox, one that still plays scratchy 45 records. Joe is purposefully early, sitting at their usual booth for two at Zula's, a restaurant in the small and impoverished border town of Nogales, their hometown. He stirs his second screwdriver with a red swizzle stick, counterclockwise, as if he can turn back the clock. The tinfoil, folded up with its secret tooth inside, is on the chipped wooden table-top. *Es de m'hijo. It's from my son.* Joe kept it by mistake. Before he could give the tooth back to Guillermo, he was called away to help with the smuggler's arrest and processing, and then Joe forgot he'd pocketed the tooth. The other agents deported Guillermo and the rest of the immigrants before Joe could return the harmless keepsake. There's no way he can get the tooth back to Guillermo. He can't even create a fantasy

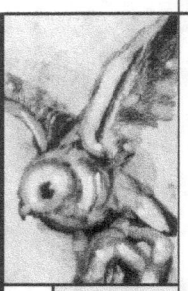

scenario where he meets the ragged man unexpectedly to return the memento, the little white tooth. The scenario that's easy to conjure is Guillermo's return home as a failure being unbearably brief and then him attempting an even more dangerous and desperate root to the US, hiking through the desert around Nogales, where the past two years has seen an over a twenty percent increase in immigrant fatalities. Security improvements are forcing more immigrants to attempt border crossings in further remote areas, forcing them to take their chances in the desert. Joe imagines Guillermo struggling through the barren, unforgiving landscape, then falling, twisting an ankle, getting lost, dying of heat exposure, or as has been increasingly the case, he sees Guillermo falling prey to bandits, armed Mexican nationals, or a double-crossing smuggler he paid as a guide, his body never to be found. Last winter, bandits shot a group of immigrants in an area just west of Nogales, inside the expansive and desolate Tohono-O'odham Reservation. Joe helped carry one of the rescued survivors to an ambulance, an older Nicaraguan woman who had her left ear blown off. After receiving baseline medical care she was sent back to Nicaragua.

Joe checks his watch. She's late. He turns the swizzle stick again. Today was another worst day in a litany of worst days; still his job has an inexplicable hold on him, a job that says more about him than he cares to hear. He orders a third screwdriver, which means he likely won't be driving back to his Tucson apartment tonight.

Jody Fernandez finally arrives, forty minutes late, limping to their booth. "Sorry, Joe. I had a hard time escaping from my parents' house." Her voice is rough but dampened, a crinkling paper bag as it's shaped into a ball. She wears a black long-sleeved tee shirt to cover her skinny arms and jeans that are supposed to be tight, but hang off her gaunt frame like elephant skin. Her black hair is tied up in a ponytail and her skin is pale. She's in her late twenties like Joe but looks like she could be his older sister, or an aunt. Still, she's in better shape than she was a few short months ago, before the rehab stint.

Joe gets the sense that she's not telling him the truth, but he's okay with it. Despite everything and the relapse warning signs he's supposed to watch for, they're close enough that the little lies don't equate to betrayal. Not yet, anyway. He says, "De nada. I've had a long day and I'm just sitting here. Unwinding."

Jody smiles, but won't show her teeth, which were ravaged by the year-plus of meth addiction. Meth is acidic, dries up the protective saliva, and while in the throes of the drug, the heavy users grind and clench their teeth to dust. She explained it to him once, saying *meth mouth* was like a neglected and abused engine being empty of oil but still redlining and chewing up its own gears. She says, "I see that. I guess you'll be sleeping on the couch tonight, then?"

As children, they were neighbors and best friends. Their mothers taught biology and chemistry at the regional high school and their fathers commuted to Tucson together. Joe and Jody, their names and lives almost the same until college, where both went to the University of Arizona. Jody married a physics Ph.D. student and upon graduation got a job teaching special-ed for elementary-aged children. Two years ago, after visiting her mother in Nogales, she and her husband were hit by a pest exterminator who fell asleep at the wheel and drifted over the center lines. Her husband died. Jody's right leg shattered in three places and her skull fractured, requiring a plate. She suffered from debilitating headaches for months and wasn't able to work, living but not living on disability insurance, so, like many of the hopeless locals of Nogales, she turned to meth.

Joe says, "Yeah, I think I might need to crash on your couch. Will that be okay?"

"Of course, but no puking allowed. I just cleaned the goddamn bathroom."

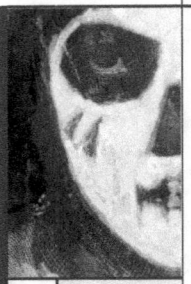

"How are you feeling?"

A waiter appears with a beer that she must've ordered before she sat down. She takes a sip big enough for the both of them, then says, "Shitty, like I was last week. But I can deal with it."

Joe fights a growing impatience. Her lateness, her short answers that aren't really answers; he knows he can't rush her back. He wants the Jody he knew before the addiction, before the accident. He might never get her back, and that's something he needs to deal with, not her.

They both order light meals, garden salads and appetizer-sized quesadillas. Joe orders another screwdriver. He says, "How's your mother?"

"Fine. Same old stuff. Bugging me to move back home until I *get back on my feet*. God, I hate that fucking phrase. Like me being able to simply walk around on my broken leg has anything to do with improving my shitty days."

Joe says, "I hate it when people say *cut a check*." As soon as he says it, he thinks the quip ill-timed and a terrible, miserable mistake. But she laughs, and he's flooded with relief, then shame because he shouldn't be so nervous around her.

Jody stops laughing, then leans forward, her head in the spotlight of the black pewter pot light fixture that hangs above their table like a bat. Her deep, brown eyes grow too big for her face. "All right, Joe, I wasn't at my Mom's house. I'm late because I found an old note from Steve, today." She smirks; a child caught doing something wrong, but not caring at all. But that's not right. She's no child and hasn't been one for a lifetime.

Joe says, "I'm sorry."

"Don't be. I'm not sure if I am. It was folded inside an old textbook, *Educational Philosophy*. My therapist keeps saying work is still a year or two away, but I've been looking through my old notes and textbooks, reading until the headaches take over."

Joe nods. He knows that's enough.

"I opened up to the chapter on cognitive disorders, and there it was, one of his wiseass notes. De-motivational aphorisms, he called them." She smiles but covers her mouth with a hand. The hand tremors and it's not enough to cover everything. "He slipped them into my notebooks and textbooks; that gloomy physics geek that he was, thinking his clever was so cute."

"What'd the note say?"

"I'll tell you if you show me what you're hiding?"

"What? I'm not hiding anything?"

"You had something out on the table and you stuffed it into your pocket when I walked over. I want to see it."

He says, "Okay. Deal. But you tell me first." Joe doesn't look forward to explaining why he has the tinfoil and what it means, but he'll play along. It's good to see her willing to play games with him, even if the game pieces aren't exactly silly.

"It said, 'Evil is a consequence of good. Cheers! Steve.'"

"That's nice. Should be a Hallmark card."

"I know. This was the only note I confronted him about. Was he implying that a gig serving special needs students was somehow a bad thing in his warped little world? He could be snotty about his field of study putting him in the supreme strata of society." Jody is talking fast, manic with her words. "If he was honest with me, if he didn't back down, he would've said something like my helping the helpless only delayed and prolonged their suffering and the suffering of their loved ones, making it all worse in the long run. He used to say shit like that at parties just to get a rise out of people. But he didn't say any of that, didn't let me put those words in his mouth. I played at being super pissed and he backed off real quick, apologizing up and down. It was the last of those notes he left in my books. Him backing down, that was my small victory, our relationship was always a competition, but now I wish he'd given me more of his pithy love-notes of doom. Isn't that sad? I spent the af-

ternoon and early evening staring at it and thinking it was all quite sad."

"It is sad. But I'm glad you can talk about it."

"Stop it. You sound like my fucking therapist when you say shit like that."

"Does she say 'cut a check' too?'"

"No, but I'll insist she do so from now on. Now pay up, Marquez. What are you hiding from me?"

"Oh oh. Using the last name, she means business."

"All business all the time."

"Okay, let's take a look." Joe takes out the tinfoil and lays it on the table. Jody furrows her brow and cocks her head to the side, and Joe panics, almost spilling his drink as he pleads with opens his hands over the tinfoil, a bumbling magician with nothing up his sleeves. He says, "Now, hold on a second. It's not what you think it is." He won't say *drugs*. He quickly launches into the story of Guillermo, fumbles through their roadside conversation, how this belonged to his son, and then how everything got so crazy that he forgot to give it back. The story already sounds rehearsed. Joe talks while slowly unwrapping the package, careful not to make any new folds or marks in the tinfoil, preservation somehow being of the upmost importance.

Jody leans over the table. "Well, what is it?"

He lifts the plastic bag, dangles it from his finger, and holds it across the table. "It's a tooth. His son's baby tooth. See? I feel bad, it's probably the first tooth he…"

Jody stands up, jumps out of her seat, and her head crashes into the pewter pot light fixture, sending its weak light arcing elsewhere into the restaurant.

"Whoa. You okay?"

She turns away from the flickering light and from him, and says, "I need to go to the bathroom." The light shines directly in his eyes, then away, then back, and Joe is unable to watch her progress through the restaurant and bar.

The waiter appears with their food, and steadies the swaying light fixture. The quesadillas are smoking and hissing on the pan. Joe wraps the little tooth back into the foil. Jody didn't just go to the bathroom; she fled from the table. He's not sure what he did, but clearly it was wrong, and he's not sure if Jody is coming back. He waits, elbows on the table, hands making a steeple, and now she has been gone long enough that he considers going to the bathroom or the parking lot to find her.

She does come back, walking as fast as her limp allows, and she sits down abruptly, the final word to some inner conversation. She stabs her fork around the salad, into the cherry tomatoes, and doesn't place her napkin on her lap.

Joe says, "Hey, everything okay? I'm sorry if…"

"Jim Dandy," she says, but doesn't look at him.

Everything has become so difficult between them. He knows he's not being fair, but these bi-weekly dinners are becoming as tedious and futile as his job. He isn't helping anyone, isn't improving lives, if anything he's making everything worse; he is that note from Steve. He orders another screwdriver.

For now, Joe won't ask Jody what's wrong because he's afraid of making it worse, and he's also being selfish. He drank too much to drive home and he needs her couch tonight, not further complications.

THEY WALK THE two blocks to Jody's one-bedroom apartment. It's late, a weeknight, and no one else is out, the streets as desolate and windswept as the desert. They don't talk. She doesn't ask Joe why he still has that tooth, why hasn't he just pitched it and moved on. Joe assumes she's just accepted it, like he has.

Her apartment is maniacally clean, antiseptic, and it smells of cleanser and air-freshener. The hardwood floor in the living room gives way to yellowed and curling

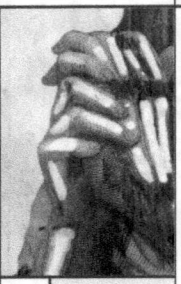

linoleum tile in the kitchen. Joe falls onto the couch in front of the TV and turns it on. Jody says that she has a headache, and disappears into her bedroom, closing and locking the door.

Joe kills the lights and tries watching a baseball game between two teams he doesn't like, then shuts off the TV and reclines, sinking into the couch, and stares at the stucco ceiling. The buzz of alcohol fills the sensory void, droning in his ears and jostling his equilibrium. He closes his eyes, the room spins, he sinks deeper into the couch, and he can't sleep. He's always had trouble sleeping. As a kid, he'd lie awake for hours and obsess over his nightmares. Then he learned to trick himself to sleep. He created and choreographed his own waking-dream, some simple innocuous scene on which to focus and loop in his head until it relaxed him enough and he fell sleep.

Tonight, in Joe's crafted dream, he gets off the couch and walks into the kitchen, first pausing above the room's borderline, where the hardwood meets the cracked linoleum. He fills a glass with tap water and drinks half, dumps the rest in the sink, then walks back to the couch, lies down, then starts it all up again, past the borderline and back to the kitchen again for his same glass of water. On one of his return trips to the sink, Joe stops filling his glass. To his right and next to Jody's bedroom is the study, and its door is open. There's no light, everything is dark, but inside the study is somehow darker than the rest of the apartment. A child, a little boy, stands in the doorway, his hands in the pockets of his jeans, hangdog in his posture. It's too dark to see any facial features, but he knows this boy. Then Joe is standing in the doorway although he doesn't want to be there, just wants to be back at the sink, filling his glass of water and make it half-empty. The boy is still in the doorway too, and he wraps his arms around Joe's legs. The embrace is brief and weak, a butterfly wing hug, and then the boy puts his hand inside Joe's and it feels like a small,

cool stone. The boy leads Joe back to the couch. There's more light here, stray neon and streetlight amber filter through the windows. The boy has thick, black hair and eyes like Jody's but not Jody's. Joe lies on the couch. He doesn't want to lie on the couch. He's tired of doing so many things that he doesn't want to do, that he can't do. The boy smiles like Jody too, hiding his mouth behind quivering lips. It's not a smile, it's something else, recognition maybe, or acceptance, whatever it is, it's filled with more despair than the tears to come. Then the boy does part his lips, those rusted hinges, and opens his mouth, and the teeth, an angler fish at the bottom of the deep, black ocean, his *teeth*, the stalactites and stalagmites of nightmare, angry shards of glass with thick tips curved in awkward and dangerous directions, teeth just spilling out of the boy's mouth. He climbs on top of Joe, sits on his lap, and tears the size of gumdrops fall from the boy's eyes as if he doesn't know he's a monster, and it's not fair because he's not supposed to be the monster, does not deserve to be the monster. But the teeth, the *teeth*.

TWO WEEKS PASS like most time does, without any acknowledgement. It's the night before Joe is to return to active duty. He is again at their booth at Zula's. He sits, a tumbleweed without a breeze, and he stares at his empty screwdriver and empty cup of coffee.

After he fled her apartment for his car and I-19, Joe was stopped at the Tubac checkpoint, his non-permanent checkpoint. The agents shined flashlights in his face. He knew they initially only saw a Mexican behind the wheel, and Joe knew he looked just like the men in that decaying trailer, dark skin, squinting and hands held empty and up. The agents were going to pat him down and take the tinfoil away, but the flashlights turned off as they did recognize their coworker. Yeah, they knew him, and they knew he was drunk. They didn't arrest him, but they didn't allow him to drive home and there was an incident report filed with the Tucson office. His immediate two-week suspension was the result.

Joe's drink and coffee cup remain empty no matter how hard he stares at them, as empty as his booth at Zula's. He knows Jody isn't coming. He didn't really expect her to show.

For two weeks, he only left his apartment to go the liquor store. He ate meals only when he wasn't drinking, and the meals consisted of slices of American cheese, cold hot dogs, dry cereal, pretzel sticks. He removed all of the curtains and shades from his windows, and at night, turned on all the lights. He drank himself into unconsciousness, and then didn't wake until late afternoon. He lay on the couch or on the floor and wouldn't sleep in his bedroom, convinced he'd find the little boy sitting at the foot of his bed, and the boy wouldn't say anything and wouldn't look at Joe, but he also wouldn't leave, not this time. He kept the tinfoil. He called Jody when he was awake past midnight. She didn't answer and didn't return his calls.

Joe leaves the booth and the restaurant, and walks to her apartment. This night is hotter than all the previous nights, and Joe sweats through his white tee shirt. Her door isn't locked and he lets himself in without knocking. Inside, the apartment is dark and a disaster of clothes and food and trash. It's as though the spotless apartment he saw two weeks ago never existed, or maybe the duration between visits was longer than those arbitrary and government-assigned weeks, time enough for the apartment to fall into such an advanced state of decay, maybe a collection of years, lost years, had passed, or epochs only measurable by fossilized bodies, bones, and teeth.

"What are you doing here?" Jody's voice is frayed, an exposed wire, quick with its electricity but weak enough that it'll break or flame out at any moment.

Joe steps over the rubble of her apartment. The place smells of sweat and burnt chemicals. Joe walks inside the study. Jody

sits on the floor, cross-legged, huddled next to a small fire, a mini-pyre set up on the hardwood floor stained black. Mounds of papers, books, and photographs surround her and the fire. She wears a white bra and black underwear along with black marks that are either bruises or smudged ash. She's too thin. Her bones are a story written in Braille, but the story is too big and horrible to be contained by her skin. Joe puts a hand into his pocket, touches the tinfoil, and he knows how she spent their time apart, and he knows this is all his fault.

Jody's eyes can't focus, and they roll around the room. Her breaths are fast and irregular as are her twitchy movements. She says, "You still have it, don't you, Joe. You still have it..." Her voice trails into whispers, and the words come too fast, fumbling over each other, letters placed inside of letters, making new sounds.

He says, "I do."

"You didn't forget to give the tooth back, you kept it on purpose, you made it all up, that story you told me is bullshit, all bullshit, you kept it on purpose. You didn't forget, no way, no way you forgot."

"I did forget, Jody."

She laughs. Then says, "Look at this. Another note. Misery is manifold, Joe. It's true. Steve wrote that on this letter over here, and

stuck it in my English Lit book, it's right over here. There. You wanna read it?" Jody picks up a slip of paper and drops it into the fire. Jody turns toward him, and her hair is frayed thread. She smiles, shows her meth mouth, her teeth, blackened and decayed, pieces missing, an incomplete jigsaw puzzle, jagged and eroded canyon boulders, each tooth or what was a tooth is a bombed and burnt-out building that cannot be repaired.

"You know what? A tooth fell out last night, Joe. It was cracked and loose, and I played with it, wiggled it around with my tongue and fingers, like we did when we were kids, I wiggled it, pulled on it, and it hurt a little but not much, nothing I couldn't take, nothing I couldn't deal with, and it just kinda popped out. Do you wanna see it, Joe? I saved it for you because you're collecting teeth now, right?"

Joe needs to do something, say something, anything that will close her terrible mouth. "I don't know why I kept the tooth. I don't know why I do what I do, anymore."

"You're a junky, just like me." She smiles again, flashes her intimate, private devastation. "Like me, Joe. See? Get that fuckin' tooth out of your pocket, you fucking junky, the worst kind, the one who won't ever admit there's a problem even when the signs, the signs, the signs are there, big as fucking billboards, billboards in your pocket, fuck billboards, a headstone, headstone in your pocket, Joe, you have a headstone in your pocket, Joe. Joe, fucking, Joe, take it out, tell me what is says, what does it say? I know what it says but I want you to tell me, I want you to tell me tell me tell me tell me..."

Joe says, "I'm sorry, Jody. I didn't mean to do this to you, to us. I'd forgotten about him. Really, I did."

He isn't strong enough to tell her that he forgot on purpose and that he worked at it and that he was good at it, better than she was, and it's why she's like she is now and it's why he's like he is now. He wants to run out of her apartment, to run away, as he's always been running away even if he never left home, where there's still room enough to hide, there's an all-encompassing desert in which to hide.

AT THE SOUTHWEST edge of Nogales, there was a stretch of desert near the border—and at the time, almost twenty years ago, a generally unsupervised border—where local teens would ride their dirt bikes and mountain bikes during the day and then later reconvene at night to light fires and bottle rockets and drink cheap six-packs. Joe and Jody were only eight and not allowed to go to there, but they went anyway. They told each set of parents they were riding to the playground for the afternoon and then would ride their bikes to the edge of the desert.

It was late afternoon, the sun low and lazy in the west, a half-shut eye, and they were knee deep in their summer routine; climbing on rocks, turning over smaller stones looking for scorpions and small lizards, filling small burrows with sand and dried grass. Two high school-aged kids on dirt bikes showed up in their desert, kicking up dirt and filling the air with their engines' whine. Jody pulled Joe behind a rock, their roles shifting from desert explorers to spies, skulking around and hiding behind boulders and saguaro cactus.

The dirt bikes were chipped-paint and dented metal. The riders didn't wear helmets. One kid was white, short and pudgy, wore a sleeveless black tee shirt with a bald eagle that was all talons and beak, and he had a mop of unkempt, dark hair, like a dead tarantula on his head. The other teen was a blonde beanpole with a crew cut, wearing a baggy white tee shirt with large, slashing letters and baggier shorts that hung down to his shins when he stood up on his pegs. The teens rode up a ridge that was one hundred yards or so away, a ridge that may or may not have been a part of Mexico, and then back down.

Joe and Jody didn't say anything or do anything, afraid of the teens, but both secretly wished for the thrill of being caught, of

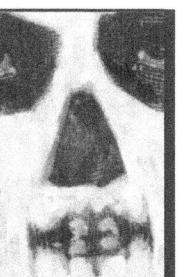

having to jump on their bikes and then somehow outrunning the dirt bikes, cutting through yards and short cuts that only they knew. They moved carefully, exchanging cactus for boulder, and crept closer to the ridge.

While tearing through another run, the chubby kid grabbed his left shoulder like it'd been stung, then swerved, and jumped off his bike, which landed on its side and slid halfway down the ridge. Three Mexican boys popped up from behind a boulder at the ridge's crest; two kids threw rocks and a third pointed and shouted something, then they all took off running down the other side of the ridge. The blond sped over and helped get his friend's bike back on its wheels. Their conversation was animated and brief. The bikes' engines were too loud for Jody and Joe to hear anything.

The teens went over the ridge. Jody pulled Joe from out of their hiding spot and said, "Come on!" She ran ahead, and he followed her up the ridge. They stopped at the top and could see everything below.

The three boys alternated fleeing with throwing their small stones at the circling dirt bikes. The teens swore and shouted epithets from the top of their mechanical steeds, and they both cradled a rock in the crook of one arm. The smallest and presumably the youngest trailed far behind the other two retreating boys. The teens focused on the straggler, tightening their circle, revving their engines and spraying dirt on the boy with their spinning, angry tires. The boy was trapped and crying, and scrambled onto a large, jagged boulder. He shouted to his friends, cupping his hands over his small mouth, but they hadn't stopped running, were too far ahead to hear his pleas. The chubby kid, the one with the eagle tee shirt, threw his rock and hit the boy in the back of his thigh. There wasn't much behind the throw, but the boy lost his balance, windmilled his arms, and fell off, behind the craggy rock, out of view of Jody and Joe.

The teens didn't stop to investigate. They tightened their formation, parallel to each other, shared an awkward high-five, and rode triumphantly back up the ridge. Joe and Jody crouched, praying they wouldn't be seen, or they'd be next, chased down the ridge, into Mexico, and then knocked off a boulder, but the teens didn't see them and didn't stop. They sped away, out of the sand, and onto the main drag and out of sight.

Silence, the voice of the desert, replaced the screaming boys and dirt bikes. Joe and Jody listened and watched for a sign from the boy who fell and there was none. They waited. The sun drooped lower in the west. The other two boys did not come back for their friend.

Jody and Joe climbed down the ridge. They crept behind the jagged boulder and found his body, lying adjacent to the flat rock upon which he landed. The boy looked like Joe and the boy looked like Jody, but only smaller, younger. The left side of his head was dented, caved-in, and was missing a flap of scalp. His left arm was held out stiffly and twitched, beating like one wing of a broken hummingbird. The lower half of his face had crumbled, ice cream melting over a cone. He was breathing, but irregularly. They crouched, hands over their mouths, but not over their eyes. His chest inflated sharply, then deflated slowly, a sagging balloon. The right side of his face was perfect, asleep. His left eye was swollen shut, or missing. It was hard to know for sure with the orbital socket broken, pushed in, along with the area around his temple. Everything leaked slowly. There were too many colors on his face. And his teeth, his *teeth*, they were baby teeth, as small as seeds, and they peppered the sand and dirt around his head, miniature headstones in the sand. Then there was one long sigh and the boy stopped breathing and his arm stopped moving.

HIS SUSPENSION IS over but Joe does not report to the Tucson office in the morning. He manages to drive his Jeep into the Tohono-O'odham Reservation and into its desert despite his near total exhaustion, his

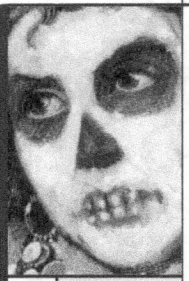

being purposefully drunk, and the pain that fills his head. He deposits a mix of aspirin, ibuprofen, and little blue pills he took from Jody's apartment into his dry, copper mouth, and grinds them up as best he can. It hurts to chew, but he won't use his water yet; he needs to conserve it.

He stops the Jeep in approximately the same area where he helped rescue the Nicaraguan woman, but he didn't save her. He knows he hasn't saved anyone and can't save anyone. This trip into the desert isn't about saving anyone. He's going to find Guillermo and give the man back his son's tooth. Joe crawls out of his Jeep and walks, slowly, due south, toward the border. He doesn't have a compass, but he thinks he knows where the border is.

Joe allows himself to remember that day in the desert. He remembers the slow walk back to their bikes, their pile of metal and chains, and the ride home. They didn't tell anyone about what had happened, didn't tell anyone about the boy. They were afraid of the teens, afraid people would think it was their fault, afraid because they were only eight and didn't know what to do. They didn't tell anyone about their desert silence.

The sun is only beginning its climb in the east, but it's midday hot. Joe's pulse throbs in his temples and inside his cheeks. His backpack of meager supplies already feels too heavy.

There was never any word or news about the little boy. They did not go back over the ridge and to that boulder. They didn't talk about it, didn't make up stories about coyotes dragging the boy away, didn't fool themselves into believing he was alive, didn't discuss the possibilities or probabilities of the police finding him or the teens coming back for the body or the boy's friends and family laying belated claim and bringing him back to Mexico. They didn't turn the boy into a legend for the neighborhood kids, didn't tell anyone that the boy might still be there. They agreed to forget, their secret, bury it inside themselves, beneath as much passed time as they could.

Despite the heat and his headache, which is a fire inside his brain, Joe walks for hours until the sun is directly above him and discerning direction becomes impossible. He finds a Desert Ironwood and sits under its thin canopy, desperate for shade. Half of his water supply is already gone. Joe takes off his small backpack, drinks, and again goes back to that day all those years ago in another part of the same desert. Joe remembers the urge to pick up the boy's teeth, those headstones, and put them in his pocket, an urge as inexplicable now as it was then.

There are teeth in his pocket now; a small one lovingly wrapped in tinfoil, and another tooth, it's adult and big and ugly with roots like talons, and that tooth is not wrapped in tinfoil or anything that would protect it. Neither tooth is his.

Joe fights waves of dizziness and nausea. His fistful of pills isn't helping. His gums are still bleeding and his right bicuspid is loose. If he pushes on the tooth with enough force there's a wet sucking sound inside his mouth. There are pliers in his backpack. Earlier this morning, the pain was too much. Unlike Jody, he couldn't deal with the pain, to where it went, and he stopped pulling on the tooth. He'll try the pliers again later, maybe when the sun goes down and when the pills kick in.

Joe falls in and out of sleep throughout the afternoon and the temperature begins to drop. Maybe a quarter of a mile beyond his tree is a ridge, and just beyond that ridge is Mexico, he's sure of it, and despite everything, he's sure he can make it over that ridge. And maybe he'll be strong enough to make it through the desert, his desert, and give back the teeth. ☙

Paul Tremblay is the author of the novels *The Little Sleep* and the forthcoming *No Sleep Till Wonderland* (2010); the fiction collection *Compositions for the Young and Old*; and the novellas *City Pier: Above and Below* and *The Harlequin and the Train*. His fiction has appeared in *Razor Magazine, Last Pentacle of the Sun,* and *Best American Fantasy 3*. He has served as fiction editor of *Chizine*, as co-editor of *Fantasy Magazine*, and as co-editor of the *Fantasy, Bandersnatch,* and *Phantom* anthologies. Paul is also a juror for the Shirley Jackson Awards.

Bruise for Bruise

BY ROBERT DAVIES

ILLUSTRATION BY DANIEL DUNCA & MARILYN VOLAN

IN WHICH IT'S A
TOWN FULL OF
LOSERS ~ ARE WE
PULLING OUT OF
HERE TO WIN?

JOSS COFFINGTON CAME to Promise to find the girl with God on her back.

He had heard many rumors about the strange town before, and had passed along a few he had made up when he was on his sixth or seventh beer, but it wasn't until he heard that particular rumor, that of the bruised girl, that he finally took to walking. He wasn't alone on those dusty back roads, either, and most of them that crowded Joss on the road were going to see the girl, too, going to the town of Promise, where monsters were born.

Some said it was contaminated well water or rainbow glinting oils that shimmered on the creek, drowned ill spirits or chemicals that spurred the blood to strange, unseen designs. Others claimed it was unseen radiation pulsing from the new power lines that snaked across the sky, trailing alongside the highway between here and there. Still others said it was simply divine will made flesh, a harsh judgment made upon a town founded by

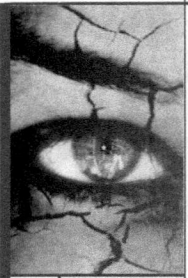

sinners when the country was being born. Perhaps it was without any reason at all, but each passing year saw strange folk filling the small houses and narrow roads of Promise, united only by their differences, untouched by the world beyond.

The birth rate in Promise was low—snake-belly low to be precise. Whether the fault lay in the seed or in the womb, none could say; but, in those jackpot moments when life found root, the town of Promise could be sure of one thing: after nine months of morning sickness and sibilant prayer, something never seen before would be spilled screaming into the world, or silent as the case may be.

Sometimes there would be something of the mother in the child, and sometimes something of the father; there was always something of the town. Leathery wings sprouted oftentimes, as common as fingers. Fur of every hue. Horns and scales were plentiful, too. Lots of feathers and thorns and glass and steel. Beneath the apple trees and the pine, anatomy was negotiable. Anything was probable. Every now and then, though, the tired wet nurses, long inured to the strange fecundity of flesh, would whistle in awe as they lifted a newborn from the amniotic slime.

Something truly special would be seen.

The Eddington triplets were each born with an extra mouth on their foreheads; the better to sing His praises, Father Quine had said, smiling. Justice Peck arrived, took two deep breaths, and burst into silent blue flame. The great-granddaughter of Old Khoas was born flower-faced and her every breath was a yellow cloud of pollen. Jirrup the Younger emerged limbless and scaled, and like the original beast his eyes were eyes of gold. The blind watchmaker's daughter Undulia grew monstrously fat and fetid as she approached her blessed day. She spilled her blue-eyed daughter in a ruinous, thick tide. To the shock of all, this newborn daughter, grunting and wailing, then gave birth to another smaller girl the size of a fist, swollen with child. This last tiny daughter, still nameless, still shivering with the chill outside the womb, stood shakily and birthed a finger-sized son whose wormy penis dragged on the floor.

Ruth's twin brothers, Luke and Persistence, came into the world in a crimson flood, the jagged steel knives growing out of their fingers and cruelly hooked thumbs must have sorely treated their mother's insides. She had survived, though it had been doubtful considering the blood that had come that December morning, and it was this improbable survival that made her someone of consequence in the town, with handsome Father Quine singling her out as a model of right living and righteous prayer.

Ruth Mingleton, however, seemed plainer than milk when she came two years later. Excitement and congratulations for a healthy girl quickly gave way to uneasy smiles and averted eyes, until soon the townsfolk were crossing the street to avoid the Mingletons and their enigmatic child. Ruth was one of the untouched, it seemed—a curiosity in a town of curiosities.

Ruth's father was let go from the sawmill; later that week, he was let down from the wobbling rafters of their ancient barn, his pants filled and his throat maroon. Her two brothers, her mother and Ruth kept to themselves then, the pale blue curtains drawn, the doors bolted. They seldom ventured into the town save for the Sunday sermons of Father Quine, though they sat at the very back, and for the necessary staples of whisky, gossip, and salt. They helped keep the glass smith in business, so it seemed, as their windows were often shattered by stones; the perilous, unkempt lawn in front of their house came to glitter in the moonlight.

They lived like that for years until Luke and Persistence snuck away one night and got themselves hitched to the passing Carnival of Blood and Thunder, which was keen on upgrading its freak show. But too much cheap whisky, an aversion to cayenne, and too many fistfights over the insatiable and mercurial Lobster Girl finally got them fired on the outskirts of Biloxi in a thunderstorm, and they came back to the town, heartbroken, penniless, and sullen as ever.

And so the story has it that it came in the darkest part of night, with a hammer and with nails and with hands that wielded them with a feral mastery. Down through the ceiling, or up through the floor, one could not rightly say. It came upon Ruth on the eve of her thirteenth birthday and made her anew. It found the bruises beneath her skin and made of them a poetry. It found the songs in her bones and made them break. It found the angel she saw on the tain and ruined its pale and perfect skin.

Ruth Mingleton didn't even cry.

She awoke to find bluish yellow smears spread across her skin—an image of a thorn on her cheek, a suggestion of velvet wings on her stomach, a golden hint of the lip-stained Grail on her inner thigh. The bones beneath her skin only accentuated the designs: her breathing would give flight to a seabird on her right shoulder; the shift of her jaw would rock the ark on her throat.

It was Ruth's mother that brought the bruises to the attention of Father Quine.

Dressed in the perfect fuligin of faith, Meticulous Quine sported great, snowy wings, just like ancient Uriel of the Scarred Palms. His black eyes glinted, and his voice was honey. He saw something in the bruises that most others did not. Ruth's mother saw it, too. They prayed together.

The townsfolk quickly took interest in Ruth then, began to murmur that she had finally revealed the gift of her birth. Of course, many claimed they had known all along that Ruth was special, revealing the hidden bits of wisdom they had hoarded for years, awaiting this day of revelation. Others, mostly those left-handed it must be said, still expressed doubt, but they were quickly silenced by the knowing frowns of Father Quine or the squinting glare of Ruth's mother. Ruth's brothers would shake their glinting fingers and make them ring.

The excitement in the town waned rather quickly, what with the coming of the harvest and the promise of another deep, implacable winter.

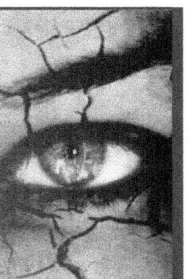

It was then that the breathtaking bruise of the thrice-nailed Christ across her back appeared. While the lesser transgressions on Ruth's arms and legs quickly healed, the Christ refused to fade. Indeed, He seemed to gain solidity with every passing day, and the stony dust of Golgotha circling her waist sprouted pale yellow flowers that glistened when she sweat.

The townsfolk crowded the narrow lane to the Mingleton's house from sunrise to dark, pleading for a chance to see, perhaps to touch, whispering and pointing out those that had thrown stones or foolishly spoken ill words before.

The pilgrims came soon after.

They came first from the outlying tobacco farms and corn fields, and then neighboring towns and fishing villages, and then from those distant states where truth can be a crime. Some carried the heavy riches they had acquired, eager to lay them before Ruth; others came with only scraps of cloth wrapping their bloody feet and foreign tongues in their mouths. One and all they came for the daughter of bruises and the stories on her skin.

Father Quine and the town elders ordered a scaffold and stage of rough-hewn wood to be erected on the Common, on the very spot where a meteorite fell in the time before trees. Blood-red tents quick sprung up around the scaffold, followed hawkers' tables and kiosks and craft-laden blankets until the entire common resembled a harvest fair. Meaty smoke rose from hissing, snapping cooking fires. Brightly colored pennons snapped. They built the ticket booth on the distant edge of the Common. To lessen the taint of commerce around such a profound miracle, Father Quine had said. Great lengths of yellow rope were strung up to form an orderly queue, snaking back and forth across the trampled grass.

Luke and Persistence collected the golden tickets at the foot of the stairs at the side of the stage, spearing them with their jagged fingers. At the ticket booth, Ruth's mother counted the money, each coin like a rosary bead in her calloused hands. Father Quine passed through the crowds nibbling on sugared insects, looking about with unconcealed pride, his wings stirring the warm, summer air.

Ruth sat on a stool at the center of the stage, a flask of warm water by her feet. She wore denim shorts and a thin white shirt that barely covered her tiny breasts. It was ripped open in the back, the better to reveal the bruised face and chest of the crucified Christ.

Nobody ever asked, but the bruises did hurt her. Each new one ached to the very heart of the bone. Sometimes Ruth awoke with a cracked rib, her breath piercing like a knife. Sometimes she awoke only to faint away from the nauseous pain writhing beneath her skin. Still, she would sit patiently on her stool as the sunburned pilgrims bought their tickets, formed a line, and ascended the stairs to examine her flesh. Lesser, smaller bruises appeared daily on her wrists and throat, her feet and her belly, her breasts, but the pilgrims hardly noticed these scenes from forgotten pages of the Bible and those other books.

They had come only for the Christ.

At the end of the day, Ruth's mother would climb the stairs and lead her back home, Luke and Persistence following a few steps back. Ruth always trembled as she walked, her legs grown stiff, her stomach empty. A few of the more pious pilgrims would trail behind the Mingletons and gather in small groups outside their house; some took to picking up the shards of glass that still littered the lawn, placing them on the tongue and swallowing them. But all the curtains were drawn tight, and in time the darkness and the silence would urge the pilgrims to move on.

Her mother examined Ruth every evening, her calloused hands flexing as she traced the fading lines of bruises and injured flesh. She marked which bruises were fading, and which were still visible. When she was done, truly done, she sent Ruth to stumble onto her mattress. Ruth slept, but she never dreamed.

After two weeks on the stage, Ruth hardly saw the pilgrims anymore as they passed before her. The pain of her new bruises and splintered bone paled beneath the simple, dull ache of sitting there, pilgrim by pilgrim, hour upon hour, sunrise until sunset. The sun burned her skin. Insects bit her eyelids and buzzed in her ears. Through it all, her bruises shone with vitality, in strange, curious shapes that beguiled the eye.

So, of course, Ruth did not notice when Joss Coffington stopped before her, and she did not hear when he stifled a cry. Only after several moments did she realize he stood there at all, his shadow shielding her from the blinding sun. He did not look at her wounds; he was looking at her face, at her.

"I love you," he said. He stood there, unmoving. Ruth looked up and caught a glimpse of his face before he was ushered off the stage by the stern-faced Father Quine.

Ruth was not so complacent after that. She started to look at the pilgrims as they came to see her, looking into their faces for something, making some uncomfortable, making some regret. Father Quine suggested a hood, and her mother agreed; but a few days later a crown of thorny bruises circled Ruth's brow, with glinting red berries of blood, and the hood was forgotten and the ticket price was raised.

Joss Coffington returned, day after day, ignoring the dark looks of Father Quine and Ruth's mother, ignoring the increasing cost as they tried to dissuade him. He paid whatever they asked and climbed the stair to stand before her, shielding her from the hot sun, if only for a moment. Most days he said nothing. On others, he again professed his love for her. Sometimes he smiled, but it seemed quite difficult for him to do. He always stood until he was forced off the platform by Father Quine or one of Ruth's brothers.

So it came to pass that on one of those

August days that made you curse the sun, Ruth waited on the stool, ignoring the countless pilgrims that passed by her and their pleas for healing or riches or prophecy. She was blind with agony, sweating. A large bruise on her right leg showed the epic Fall of Jericho; the whisper of angels casting down that ancient wall had nearly broken the femur in three places, so fierce was the reckoning of their angelic fury.

It was late in the day, and he had not yet come. She feared they had finally scared him off. Her mouth was dry but she did not care any longer. She almost let herself slip from the stool, let herself slip from her skin.

Father Quine's voice broke the silence, and a scuffle broke out in the line. Ruth turned to see Joss Coffington push Quine and a few pilgrims aside and dart up the stairs.

He ran to her and put his hand on her shoulder.

"You don't have to stay here," he said.

He reached down and pulled her arm, but she was immovable, inviolate in her agony. A statue would have moved more readily; but where a statue would be cool stone, she was fevered, damp flesh. She looked into his eyes.

"Go," she said. "Go, before it is too late."

Footsteps rattled the scaffold. Persistence and Luke moved forward as one. Father Quine urged them on. Persistence grabbed Joss Coffington by the collar and pulled him down, his fingers slicing into Coffington's shoulders. Luke slammed his right knee into Coffington's face with a wet crack, again and again. Persistence kicked his spine and slashed at his side. Coffington fell limp.

The crowd barely reacted. If anything, they regarded the entire event as an inconvenience, something that kept them from the momentary miracle of standing before Ruth and seeing her bruises and her pain. They had all come so far to see her. They had waited so long.

Ruth saw Joss Coffington lying on the scaffold. She sat still. Her hands opened and closed.

A silence fell on the crowd.

Ruth seemed to whisper to herself, looking down.

"What is it, child?" said Father Quine.

She whispered again.

Father Quine moved to her side, leaning down to hear.

Striking like a cobra, Ruth grabbed Father Quine's arm and he dropped to his knees. The memory of her every wound passed through her fingertips and burned into his mind. His skin grew damp and darkened with Biblical scenes. Bone snapped and feathers smoked. Reddish spittle fell from his mouth, followed by a scream. Father Quine slumped forward, his wings aflame.

Ruth stood and looked toward her brothers. "Stand back," she said, her fingertips smoldering. "I have ages within me."

Persistence and Luke stood still, shocked by her feral eyes. But their surprise gave way and as one they smiled and slowly circled her like hungry wolves. Their mother shouted from the chaotic crowd. People pushed and shoved to get out of the way, their eyes fixated on the strange tableau upon the stage. Those wise to the danger of crowds drifted away from the stage, forking their fingers and spitting twice.

The brothers lunged, but they were thrown back

Thrown back not by force, but by a look, a casual gesture. Each jerked upright, like fish upon the line, held in place by unseen chains. Dark, bruised lines slipped across their faces, across the skin of their throats; the painful lines formed angels, magi, and flibbertigibbets by the dozen. Reptilian in their speed, they shifted so quickly that it seemed the figures danced. The skin split in their wake, bleeding. The lines slowed and dissipated, leaving the brothers' sweat-sheeted skin red. Spent, they dropped to the platform, one atop the other.

Ruth's dripping hands were ruined now, tattered and charred.

She knelt beside Joss Coffington and touched his face. She listened at his mouth

for breath. Her shattered fingers trailed across his chest and found no heartbeat.

She turned to face the crowd, and her eyes held only vengeance. Not the petty vengeance of rage or jealousy, but that primordial ire that ignited the stars. Ruth found her mother and pointed directly at her, freezing her in place. Ruth's gaze took in the entire crowd, each one a celebrant, each one an idolater. Ruth shouted a word heard only in the quiet days before the caul dried on the world, and she tore her throat to shreds.

Everyone in the town felt it, though none would ever agree what had happened.

Some said it was a simple feather or the passing of warm wind over a cloudy dandelion; others said it was the touch of a lover, of a mother, of a glass-eyed stranger. Some said it felt like grass growing. Others mentioned razors, warm oil, and the cracking of a knuckle. Old Khoas said it was rust, and he was right. A few said nothing at all, but it was there in their eyes. It entered them, unfurled itself, and never left.

She opened Joss Coffington's shirt and pressed her smoldering hand against his chest. The blood spilling from her mouth sizzled when it hit her fingers. She leaned against him, putting all her weight against that hand. Her shirt fell away, and her bruises were lambent.

There was that strange wind again and Ruth stood, her eyes wild.

Joss Coffington sat up and winced. He looked up and took Ruth's waiting hand.

The mark of her hand on his chest had swollen already, the skin shiny and red. What she did to the townsfolk that day, she did to him, too, only different. Everything they were, the secrets of their blood and memories, was now in him, coiled like so many serpents, all clenched at the base of his skull like a writhing fist. He was legion.

She put an arm around him and they walked off the stage and down the stairs, heedless of the crowds around them. A few of the townsfolk knelt, reaching out to touch them as they passed. One brushed a finger against the gaping wound at Coffington's side, pulling it away with awe.

They walked out of the town, and they walked until their feet bled, and then they walked until the stars filled the sky. Those that followed after Joss and Ruth lost them in the darkness in a matter of hours. None saw them after that.

Behind them, in Promise, it took several weeks for the stories and rumors to die down. The townsfolk tried to carry on as they had before, but something was amiss. Old Khoas was the first to notice, but he said nothing. The wooden platform fell during a bad nor'easter and the town was suffocated in white. The frightened elders called a meeting on the town common and patiently waited as everyone came. The blue moonlight blackening their faces, the townsfolk listened as the wingless Quine began to speak, but his words were unnecessary. It had become increasingly clear that the wet nurses had nothing to do, and most in the town were certain they never would again. Other elders took their turns to speak, but most townsfolk had stopped listening, and alone or in small groups they drifted off into the darkness, until, at long last, there was only the bruised whiteness of the empty Common beneath the cold winter moon. ☙

Robert Davies lives in Somerville, Mass., with his wife Sara, their cats Lilith and Tiamat, and a bunch of books. His stories have appeared in *Interzone*, *Shroud Magazine*, and *Arkham Tales*. His horror novella, *Hiram Grange and the Digital Eucharist*, will be published by Shroud Publishing this year.

Court Scranto

BY CALEB WILSON

ILLUSTRATION BY STEVEN ARCHER

IN WHICH THERE
ARE MANY WAYS
A GHOST CAN
HAUNT THOSE
LEFT BEHIND

COURT SCRANTO WAS that portly kid with a bowl haircut who smelled like animal crackers as late as ninth grade. We never knew how his scent or style-sense would evolve, because on the first weekend of tenth grade he was struck and killed by a vehicle. The police guessed it was a truck, because of the bodily damage, but they never found who did it. The only evidence was his body lying there, broken, by the side of the dirt road near his family's farm. The Monday morning announcement stunned us, the pop as Mr. DuTremble in his office dropped the microphone, then his voice, hoarser than usual, and the somber message about what had happened to Court.

Court's corner of the lunchroom looked so empty that day. This was the place where he'd always sat alone. He was one notch in the hierarchy above those poor guys and girls whose names we didn't even know; just vague facts, like they had a mentally retarded brother or that they once slipped on spilled applesauce in the hall and broke a rib—they all sat together in glum rows. We knew Court's name, but he sat apart, back in the corner, beneath an angrily humming emergency exit sign.

The school held a memorial for Court. It was out front, under the flagpole, all of us sitting in tiny white folding chairs. Mr. DuTremble said some words. Carl Mock put on a rock star expression and played an imaginary drum-set on his right knee, which distracted all of us sitting within a few rows from the words of the speech.

"That is so not appropriate, Carl." It was Liz Abetti, with her saintly red hair and fiery blush. We all knew that he liked her. Carl turned bright red, too, and stopped messing around.

So we did hear the end of the eulogy, where Mr. DuTremble talked about how much Court would be missed at White River High, and how the English classes were all going to spend the next few days remembering Court in ways appropriate to our grade levels. Ninth would remember him with adverbs and adjectives, tenth through metaphor and simile, eleventh with literary allusions, and twelfth with free verse.

Although we were unsure at first that we'd have anything to say about Court at all, the memorial project quickly produced results. Mindy Shelton was the first, when on the following Tuesday she shared something with Mr. McCabe's tenth grade English class. "On the first day of ninth grade, I was so nervous, and Court's locker was right next to mine. He had a very sweet smile. He said to me, 'Don't worry, I'm nervous too.' He was the only person who talked to me the first day."

"And can you think of a simile or metaphor relating to Court?" Mr. McCabe stood with his chalk in hand, waiting to add it to the board, and if it was judged good enough, to the Court Scranto memorial mural.

"Court made my tears dry up like a stream evaporating."

"Well," said Mr. McCabe, "that's close."

Across the hall, in Mrs. Higgins's ninth grade class, Tyler Coutermarsh was remembering Court as well. "Last year in eighth grade I was walking through the parking lot after school and I saw Court walking there too. He didn't see me because I was behind him, and I saw him pick up three pieces of trash and put them in the trash bin. Oh yeah, an adjective. Um, environmental?"

Lucy Aubin compared Court to Queequeg. "He was an outsider, different than all of us, but he had dignity."

Chris Hickey said: "Lonely Court / contemplates the world / observing, watching, learning / I think he must know something that / we do not."

And these are only a few examples. All of us, school-wide, remembered Court in our own various ways. It wasn't uncommon, in the two weeks after the memorial, for us to hear each other trading Court stories in the hall between classes. Someone, nobody else saw who, hung a wreath on his locker, and certain freshmen girls like Karma Gilman and Ariana Fuller started leaving fresh flowers at the foot of it.

By the beginning of October Court Scranto was entrenched in our memories as a fallen hero, our silent sentinel who had sat alone in the corner of the room, alone not because he was aloof, but because none of us had been cool enough to sit with him.

We had a good fall break. Several groups of friends, the Phil Gidley-Michael Ferris-Burke Ryder cross-country team clique and the Erin Hunt-Dan Hadlock-Katie Kinney band clique, both held Court Scranto parties at their homes, where everyone sat in a circle and reminisced about the emptiness of his favorite seats in each school room (at the back, in the corner).

There also occurred during fall break an incident at the White River Twin Cinema, when Morgan Haines, kissing her boyfriend Nick Whalen, murmured "Court" in his ear. He stood up, spilling buttery popcorn everywhere, and shouted "How can you defile his memory like that?"

But when we returned after break things began to change. The first hint of a shift came when Rebeccah Burch told her best friend Meredith Browning about something Court once did that didn't fit the mold. "It was during gym class," she said. This conversation itself took place during Coach Scudder's gym class, and the girls had retreated behind the bleachers to avoid running the mile.

"He kissed you, didn't he?" Meredith had a filthy smile. "Was he a good kisser? I always imagined him to be."

"No, he didn't kiss me," said Rebeccah. "That's the problem. I tried to kiss him, and he told me that he was saving himself for marriage!"

"Court had principles," said Meredith. "What are you, a slut?"

"I just thought it was a little bit selfish," said Rebeccah.

The shrill of a whistle bit into their conversation. "Girls! I see you back there! I'm adding a lap!"

"Sorry, coach!"

Rebeccah's story spread rapidly through the school, though we discounted it, at first, to her jealousy. She did have a tarnished reputation, after all.

But later, over lunch, Rob Aldrich remembered another detail that didn't jibe with Court's saintly image. He mentioned this to Luc Maynard, but then waited till they had walked past the Court memorial table and added their tithe of cookies and chips to the massive pile that was gathered up, at the end of every day, by Mitch the janitor and donated to the poor.

"Well?" said Luc, after they had found seats.

"This was in Mr. Heaviside's Social Studies class. We were doing a project that had partners, making a world map. I asked Court if he wanted to be my partner, and he said no, he already had one."

"Well," said Luc, "he probably already did have one."

"Nope," said Rob. "I remember this well, because my feelings were hurt. I looked around and found another partner. I had to work with Mike Loschiavo, which sucked. But at the end, I checked, and Court didn't have a partner after all. He ended up working with Allison what's-her-name. The one who slipped in applesauce that time."

"So?"

"Don't you see?" Rob paused as Dan Hadlock, across the cafeteria, clashed his raised fists in what we called the "Scranto salute," which swept the room like a wave. He lowered his voice. "He blew me off! I mean, I know Court was a great guy. . ." His voice shrank again. "But he had a mean streak."

Luc could never keep anything to himself. The lacrosse team locker room was a hotbed of rumor. And since all the lacrosse players had serious girlfriends to whom they told everything, by the end of October everyone knew.

One morning those of us who rode the early bus saw Mitch the janitor with a paint-can and brush, kneeling in the lobby in front of Court's memorial mural.

"What are you doing?" said Randy Burch, Rebeccah's sister.

Mitch tried to stop us from seeing, but three of us, Josh Whitney, Carl Mock, and Lane Fitzgerald, tackled him, spilling his can of paint in a white tongue that lapped the linoleum. Mitch shook his head. "I didn't want you to see it. . ."

In violent red marker at the bottom of the mural, just below Court's portrait, were the words: "Heart-breaker."

In shock, we left Mitch to finish his task. The phrase had already burned itself into our collective consciousness.

Gossip divided us. There were camps, the male sports teams and the science nerds, who remained heavily pro-Court, but support among the girls took a serious hit, especially when Meredith began reminding anyone who would listen about Rebeccah's story.

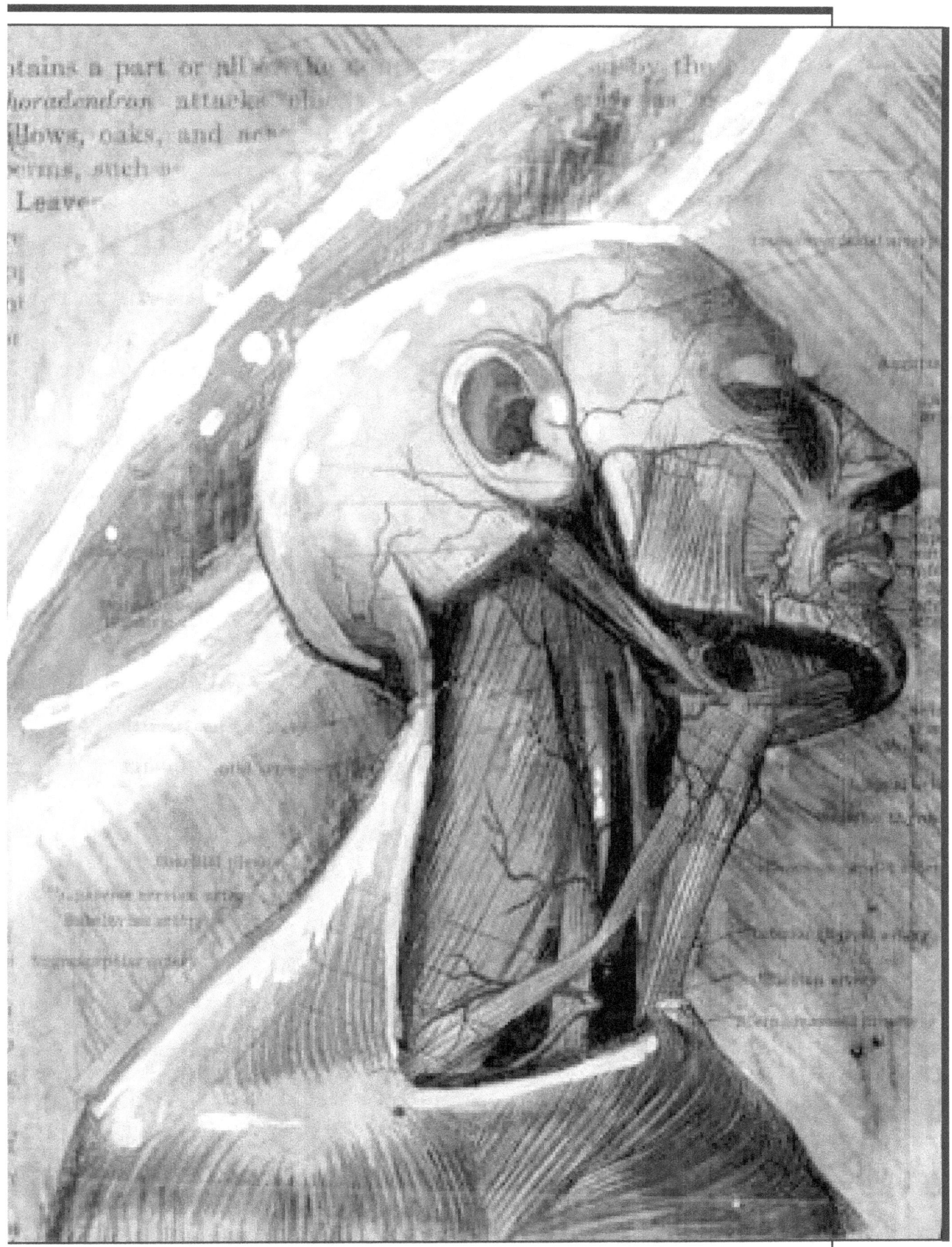

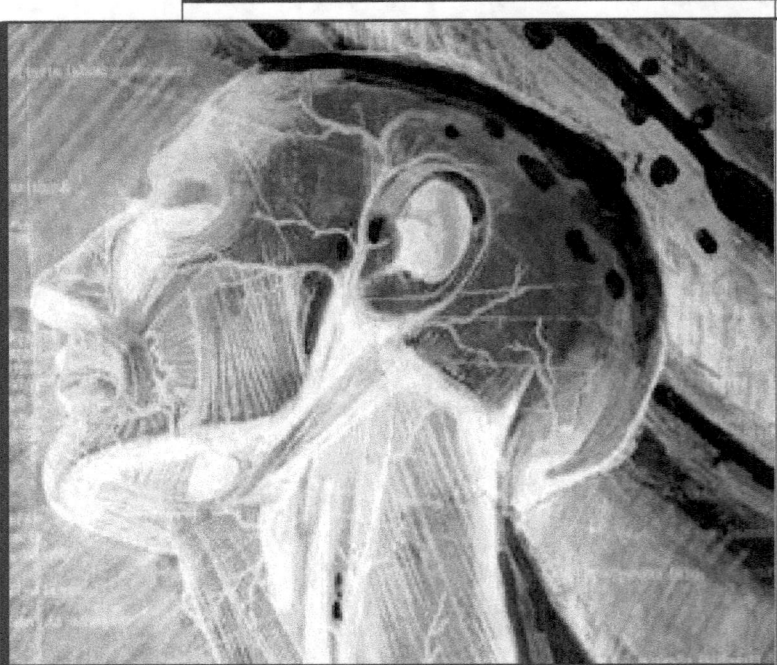

More damning anecdotes began to spread, like cancer expanding from a single metastasizing cell.

Court had asked Katie Kinney on a date and then stood her up. He had been lab partners with Karen McCabe, Mr. McCabe's daughter, and though he had drawn a killer cover for their lab report that had a very realistic and bumpy-looking frog with shadows and all, she had done all the work. She had been happy at the time, but in retrospect none of this seemed quite proper. He had borrowed Gerry Zigman's biology textbook one weekend, which meant Gerry couldn't study for the test, and then later denied ever having it at all. Gerry had to pay for it, which pretty much wiped him out for the rest the year, because his single mom was on a fixed income.

In mid-November, a few weeks after the first graffiti, someone else wrote on the memorial: "Wolf in sheeps clothing." Not only did it take Mitch two days to paint over it this time, but somebody else (Randy Burch claimed Dan Hadlock, though Dan denied it) added the missing apostrophe.

The next week Jean Harrison told a rapt lunch crowd about the time she saw Court entering one of the computer labs after school was over. She was waiting for her ride when he opened the door and slipped in. "I don't know where he got the key. He looked like he was up to no good, so I went to the other door and looked through the mesh. He had a floppy disk, and he was putting it in each drive, typing something, and then moving on to the next one."

"Oh man," said Chris Hickey. "That must have been the lab where all the computers got the virus that corrupted all our BASIC programs."

"It was," said Jenn. She shook her head. "I almost can't believe he would have done something like that."

"I can believe it." Phil Gidley took a potato chip from a ziploc bag and crunched it up, waiting for our beam of attention to swivel in his direction. "You know, I once heard a funny noise from inside Court's locker. I listened at the little grating and there were clucking sounds coming from in there."

"A chicken," said Liz Abetti. "His family owned a farm."

Phil continued. "But why would he have one in his locker, right? Well, at the end of the day, I had to stick around anyway for cross-country practice, so I decided to wait and watch and see what I could see."

"Well?" We spoke as one, on tenterhooks.

"So I'm hiding in that little shadowy alcove between the boys' and girls' bathrooms. I hear footsteps coming from around the corner. It's Court. He sets his backpack on the floor outside his locker, and takes out a knife. Wicked long and rusty. He opens the locker and picks up the chicken by the legs. There's squawking and flapping and feathers going everywhere. He goes somewhere out back behind the school but I'm scared to follow him."

"Chicken!" Nick Whalen laughed at his own joke, but the rest of us were too chilled to laugh.

"I found bloody feathers out by the old baseball diamond," said Erin Hunt.

Someone added horns and pitchfork to Court's mural portrait, and this time instead of cleaning it up, Mitch, at the order of Mr. DuTremble, just took the whole thing down. There was a blank space on the lobby wall for a few days, and then there was a trophy case.

The Court shrine at his old table in the cafeteria dwindled away too, though for a few days the outcast kids like Allison Applesauce still offered their little packs of raisins and cartons of chocolate milk. They were always several days behind the curve.

Stories about the dark side of Court flourished like fetid mushrooms. How he had muttered some cryptic words in the middle of Mrs. Lyford's Latin test and everyone except he had failed. How he always finished the mile rum in gym class, without appearing winded, minutes before everyone else. How even the teachers, when Court Scranto walked through the halls, moved to the edges with looks of subjugated terror.

Mitch fixed the buzzing exit sign that had been Court's old marker, and he took the corner table away all together. We stopped referring to Court by his full name. It became bad luck. The first casualty was Rachel Hauck. In the middle of recounting a story in which Court cursed her ball-point pen so it exploded inside her backpack, she tripped on a loose linoleum tile, fell, and found a pen just like the one in her story sticking two inches into her thigh. We thought it was safe to call him "C. S." for a while, until Michael Ferris took the initials of Court in vain while walking down the stairs, slipped, and lost a tooth.

Burke Ryder suggested "Yard," which worked until Morgan Haines broke three fingers in a slammed door. From then on, we called Court by a series of ever-shifting nicknames, "Yar," "Arr," "Argh," "Pirate," "Mate," "Old Matey."

Eventually we stopped calling him anything, as horrible accidents always seemed to result, and when we needed to invoke him we used a pause, in which we quickly knocked our fists together in a Scranto salute.

This was fine until entire rooms of the school began to be corrupted by the memory of Court. It started with Mr. Heaviside's room, where the windows turned filmy black and the chalkboard filled itself each night with row upon row of Court's blocky signature. Mr. DuTremble closed the room for the rest of the year, relocating all the classes held there to the auditorium. It was only the beginning. Mrs. Higgins's room suffered the same fate, and so did Mr. McCabe's.

By the middle of December, the lights in the cafeteria all started sounding Court's warning buzz and the vending machines dispensed nothing but animal crackers. More rooms went bad, and the hallways between them, roped off with caution tape, turned sour with memories of Court.

WE THOUGHT THAT Christmas break would let us clear our heads. We needed a new start. In a way we got one. Dan Hadlock came back from break with his hair in a bowl cut. Within two days Carl Mock and Liz Abetti shared it.

By the end of January we all had Court's haircut and had gotten used to animal cracker pudding, meatloaf, and soup. All except Allison Applesauce and her friends. They talked about us. At their table, alone, we heard them, talking, laughing. We pitied them, still, in our own way, as we chanted in unison, filling our notebooks with his name.

Court.

Scranto. ☺

Caleb Wilson's fiction has appeared in places like *Diagram*, *PodCastle*, *Lady Churchill's Rosebud Wristlet*, and *The Year's Best Fantasy and Horror*. He and his wife live in Illinois. His alter-ego works in a library.

Selected Views of Mt. Fuji, With Dinosaurs

BY HUNTER EDEN

ILLUSTRATION BY DIMITAR MARINOV

IN WHICH
SAMURAI FIGHT
DINOSAURS, AND
THAT ALWAYS
EQUALS AWESOME

I: The Pterodactyls of Nihonbashi Bridge

THIS TIME HAD a certain magic. A little under two hundred years ago, after the Shoguns closed Japan to all foreigners of whom they disapproved, the *kyoryu* wandered forth from the forests, mountains and seas. The Shogunate at first ruled the *kyoryu* demons, then gods, then demons again, then animals. Over the past century, every Japanese child had learned to identify the different types of *kyoryu*, to say which were dangerous and which merely dangerous to tease. The Three-Horned roamed the grasslands of the Kanto, trampling rice paddies and destroying barns. The long-necked Pine-Eaters herded in forests, eating the branches of conifers and cedars. The Sickle Claws hunted deer in packs, killing pigs and cattle or farmers and travelers. In Shikoku, the Dragon-Walkers pursued carts across fields and killed off the occasional platoons of cavalry the Shogun sent to drive them away.

And beside *kyoryu*, the black ships of the Dutch visited Japan as they had since the founding of the Shogunate and the isolation of the country. They insisted the *kyoryu* (or as the white foreigners said, *dinosaurussen*—"terrible lizards") had lived long ago in their homeland, but had died out. In addition, Dutch medical books brought radical new theories on the true extent of the spleen's influence on the body, and the number of lungs a healthy human being should possess. Men spoke seriously of ships that ran on hot mist, and houses lit by fiery vapors. With such wonders, what did wild reptiles matter?

Masaki and Keiji stood on Nihonbashi Bridge looking at the distant peak of Mt. Fuji. They steeped in the odor of fish as they waited for the Mad Artist. Masaki had lived for sixty years. When he was younger, he had fought the Dragon-Walkers of Shikoku. He also killed a peasant for stepping in his way. The man wasn't especially old, nor was he lame or carrying any sort of load aside from two azure fans he had been holding open, perhaps to sell. He might have been deaf. Either way, he walked in front of Masaki, neither excusing himself nor deferring as a farmer should to a samurai. Masaki cut him down, leaving him to die in the road. The man had eyes like an animal's, wide and full of one emotion at a time. Now happiness, now surprise, now pain. Masaki did as he had a right to. The needs of samurai eclipsed those of farmers.

Keiji was twenty, and he would kill a man someday too. Like most samurai, it would not be in anything like a battle. A drunken argument maybe, some imagined offense to the honor. Masaki had been nineteen when he killed the peasant. It had been before he went to Shikoku, and his hands kept sweating and shaking for an hour after he had done it. He felt proud. Then he worried about Hell.

Skin-winged *haneyube* landed on the long wooden boats in the canal. They pecked at baskets of fish before taking to the air carrying limp squid in their toothed beaks, the fishermen swearing below. Some men could train the smaller *haneyube* to sing. Not these dingy canal-dwellers, but the lighter breeds with long tails and lizard-like heads bearing manes of black fur. Masaki had seen concerts where geisha played their *samisen* and sang in accompaniment with a cage of *haneyube*. He thought it grotesque. The smell of the *haneyube* alone put him off. It was a smell of musk and flesh, an old smell. All the *kyoryu* had that scent. He remembered how in Shikoku, as he rode from a great Dragon-Walker, the entire forest took on that smell. Looking back, he saw its tiny, two-fingered arms waggling, its beady eyes set deep in the skeletal dragon face. Jaws dipped in red from the horses and men it had killed, fifteen arrows piercing its striped rhinoceros hide, its shins covered in sword cuts. . .But Masaki remembered the smell most.

The two samurai waited ten minutes before the Mad Artist arrived. He teetered on a long cane, carrying his brushes and inks strapped to his back. Even in his sixties, the Mad Artist tilted his head to the side like a young rake, smiling at ladies and sweeping aside the dead fish in his path with his bamboo walking stick. Bald, he wore no cover on his head, and dressed in a light summer *yukata* and reed sandals. He might have passed for a monk if it hadn't been for his smile and the constant tilt of his head.

The Mad Artist made prints for a living, and he would make them of anything, for anybody. *His Dream of the Fisherman's Wife*, depicting a young woman pleasured by two ammonites, hung on the walls of whorehouses across Edo. He signed his work with a plethora of names—Sōri, Taito, Hokusai, or just "Mad Artist," "The Insane Old Man." He greeted Masaki and Keiji with a quick bow that the two samurai returned.

"We begin here," said the Mad Artist, slinging down his pack and placing a vial of ink on the railing of the Nihonbashi Bridge before setting up his easel.

"Here?" asked Keiji.

The Mad Artist nodded.

"Here is our first view of Mt. Fuji," he said. "As personally requested by our patron, Otojiro-*san*."

Dipping his brush in the vial of ink, the Mad Artist began to sketch the canal, starting with the flat, snowy peak of Mt. Fuji and then moving to the great, crested *haneyube* that rode as still as kites on the high winds. He drew them as jagged slashes, picking their shapes from the low clouds and realizing them in a few, perfect strokes before deigning to draw the jostling fishmongers on the river. For some weeks, Masaki and Keiji would stand guard over the Mad Artist as he drew sketches of Fuji-*san* all over central Japan.

II: Raptor Attack on Lake Ashi

LOW-LYING FOG hung over Hakone the morning that the Mad Artist went out with Masaki and Keiji to draw Lake Ashi. Stands of pine trees bristled by the shore, poking through the mists like the top of distant Mt. Fuji through her wreath of clouds. It was hilly country around Hakone, and the houses of the villagers huddled around Lake Ashi's shores.

"Shikoku has this kind of mist," said Masaki as the Mad Artist set up his easel and inks in a clearing. "On mornings like this we saw Dragon-Walkers the height of temples, capable of swallowing a man in full armor. They came out of the mountain forests in winter and attacked the farmers with snouts like saddles and teeth the length of daggers. Monsters like that could eat all of Edo."

Keiji spat into the reeds.

"No animal could be big enough to eat a whole city," he said. "It's just not possible. You might as well tell us it breathed blue fire. Besides, what good would eating a city do?"

Masaki quieted as the Mad Artist began to draw. Both samurai wore heavier kimono in the cold mist, but the printmaker still only wore his summer *yukata*. He drew in long slashes, tapering lines that reminded the older samurai of written characters before they began to shape into houses and banks of mist. Keiji stood with one hand on the pommel of his sword. He always stood that way, and Masaki assumed at first that he just read too many stories about samurai— stories of the kind that the Mad Artist illustrated. Only little by little, traveling from Edo across Sagami province, staying at decrepit inns or sleeping in abandoned barns, did Masaki realize Keiji's embarrassment. A young samurai, he had to work for Otojiro-*san*, a lowborn publisher, guarding an elderly printmaker for less money than an Edo merchant made in a week.

Masaki didn't care, because he had no more shame. He drank his *sake*, visited the pleasure quarters, and slept in the decaying house his family left him. He had no servants to light the morning fires or make him tea, only a flock of small *kyoryu*–Lizard-Chickens with dirty brown feathers. They were harder to keep than fowl, but cheaper. Masaki's hands bore the scars of their bites. His arms had deep scratches from their kicks. Masaki's wife died three years before of tuberculosis, never giving him children. He cooked his own food when the neighbor woman didn't bring him anything. With the money he would make off this excursion with the Mad Artist, Masaki might buy something better than *kyoryu* meat, but he was too old to worry about eating well or living with anything beyond his tattered blankets and the utensils his parents' servants had used. He could sharpen knives or patch sandals when the Mad Artist needed no more sketches. If he ran out of money for whores and *sake*, he could always slit his belly.

Across Lake Ashi, duck-billed *kyoryu* ate cattails by the water's edge, their blotchy, green and brown bodies difficult to see in the mist and foliage. The Mad Artist drew them into his sketch as long arcs of black. Masaki looked up at Mt. Fuji, just beginning to resolve herself from the mist. Everything dripped, and he felt clumps of wet grass sticking to his two-toed *tabi* boots. Some-

where nearby, birds called—a low and melodious sound.

The noise seemed strange to Masaki, almost too low for a bird, but too high for any sort of *kyoryu* he had seen. It might be a *haneyube*, but they tended to sound shrill, despite the trainers' attempts to give them singing voices. This song moved from a tinkling music to a lower noise like a disgruntled cat's growl. The Mad Artist stepped back from his sketch and looked it over, adding lines to the hair-thin reeds he had painted. From the trees, the scent of the *kyoryu* drifted.

"Something's in those pines," Masaki said.

"I heard nothing," said Keiji.

"Do you smell that?"

"No," said the Mad Artist, the perpetual grin screwing off his face.

"I don't smell anything," said Keiji, drawing his sword. A soft pine twig broke, and several nostrils drew in breath.

"Hurry up with your things," said Masaki to the Mad Artist.

Three Sickle Claws burst from the forest in a spray of pine needles, the large claws on their toes out. Each had a tuft of black feathers on its head, a topknot erected to its full height before tapering down into the white and black plumage of the arms and back and the down that covered the flanks and underbelly. Long tails held their bodies balanced. The largest among them had two tails, each with a peacock-like spread of blue feathers at the end. These tail-feathers opened and closed as the Sickle Claw launched itself into the clearing, racing for Masaki.

Masaki drew his sword and slashed at the big Sickle Claw's neck. The *kyoryu* slipped away from the strike, cooing at the old samurai as it turned to face him. Masaki had fought only a few times in his life. He had been to Shikoku, and afterward fought from time to time against robbers and *kyoryu*. The only thing he ever remembered about any of his battles was that they were faster than his mind. He found himself block-

ing, striking, kicking and dodging. Each attack became a perilous giving of energy. Each blow he received sapped not his well of skill or agility, not his threshold for pain, but the belief in his ability to fight on.

Masaki struck down one of the smaller Sickle Claws with a blow that opened its throat. He twisted about, slaying another with a wide butcher's cut to the animal's spine before Keiji could reach it. But the biggest one with its strange two tails eluded him. Masaki slashed across the big Sickle Claw's shoulders, intending for its neck. It returned with a kick at the older samurai's chest. Masaki closed his eyes, expecting the *kyoryu* to hook open his ribcage. He felt the sharp prick of the Sickle Claw's talon, and then it fled back into the forest as Keiji flung several missing blows at its head. Masaki felt blood on his chest, but opening his kimono, he saw only a tiny puncture right over his heart.

The three men raced away through the foggy pines, listening for more Sickle Claws. When they slowed, Keiji walked in front with sword drawn, ashamed at his slowness in not killing the big Sickle Claw. Masaki held one hand to his chest, wondering why the creature had not killed him. Had Keiji chased it off? Perhaps, but people told legends about the Sickle Claws that made him think otherwise. Farmers said that Sickle Claws could untie knotted ropes and talk like human beings. Had the beast marked him? They walked on, and the *kyoryu* scent stayed with the old samurai, as ephemeral and distant as birdsong in a misty forest.

III: The Great Wave of Plesiosaurs

THEY CAMPED IN an abandoned temple one night on the Kanagawa coast, two months into their travels. The temple's roof stood mostly complete, although tiles had fallen in, shattering on the floor and leaving a powder like broken shells. Beneath one of the largest holes, Masaki and the Mad Artist slept beside a fire as Keiji stood guard outside. Keiji liked standing guard. It gave

him a feeling of purpose, obedience. He could stand for hours with one hand on his sword, posing stoic for nobody. They always kept watch now, because the Sickle Claw packs had followed them from Hakone, watching from beneath the trees. When he stood guard, Masaki could see the Sickle Claws pacing like wolves, and a shadow with two tails bearing peacock-like feathers. The wound on his chest remained a scar, a tiny coin of white flesh.

Now Masaki lay back on his bedroll, holding his sword to his chest. The Mad Artist slept in silence. The old samurai closed his eyes, but couldn't slip away from the temple. The dripping sound of the fading fire and the noise of mice and lizards scampering through the roof tiles above him stayed in his head.

Some Shintō priests said that the storm god Susano'o made the *kyoryu* to parody people. Ponderous Dragon-Walkers with their tiny, atrophied arms represented shoguns, powerful enough to step on anything but unable to reach their own mouths to feed themselves. They called the Three-Horned, "the farmers of heaven," for they constantly dug and trampled the earth, grazing on crops. The bald-headed, scrawny *haneyube* were Buddhist monks, flying high above everything but coming down to pick at dead fish like everybody else. Sickle Claws with their talons, feathers and bird-like necks became the Gods' answer to poor samurai: always hunting, killing as much from pride as hunger.

The Buddhists said that *kyoryu* were all reincarnations of men. According to the monks, farmers whose fields had been burned became the Three-Horned, and robbed fishmongers became the *haneyube*. Shintō priests became the little Lizard-Chickens that the poor raised for food. "That," said the Buddhists. "Is the justice of heaven. They fed the people offal while alive, and now they feed the poor with their flesh." The Shintō priests debated this theory vehemently.

Masaki, like most Japanese, believed in both faiths. He thought little about where the *kyoryu* came from. It didn't matter to him.

They were just more animals, common as cats in the street. Little Sickles—the *kyoryu* that looked like Sickle Claws but didn't grow as large—scavenged trash in the yards around his house. Sometimes the neighborhood boys would trap one and kill it with spades and hoes, taking its claws and leaving a mess of blood and gray feathers.

But *kyoryu* always produced that smell, the smell he caught on the wind whenever he knew the Sickle Claws followed the Mad Artist's troupe. The same musty, sad odor that nearly made him sick in Shikoku. Sometimes he awoke to that scent, unsure if it came from some tiny *kyoryu* that had snuck into his decaying house or from the larger beasts that hunted in his dreams. He smelled it everywhere and lay on his back, praying to the compassionate Buddha Amida to bring back the scent of wood fires burning through the thin winter air or the summery smell of grass. If he prayed long enough, it usually went away. But sometimes he smelled *kyoryu* for days, and wondered how others didn't. He smelled it in Shikoku and on this journey with the Mad Artist. He smelled it the moment he cut between the shoulders of the peasant in Edo, and a stray Lizard-Chicken scurried past his feet. He smelled it as he kicked aside the fans the man carried, and looked into his deep, animal eyes.

FROM THE SEAS off Kanagawa one could see Mt. Fuji very clearly, even on a gray, stormy morning like the one on which the Mad Artist and the two samurai sought to look at her. Standing on the rocky beach, they scanned the heaving water. The sea had a deep and fearsome shade of blue like the night, with curling white claws of foam gouging at the sky. The fishermen sat ashore, readying their boats and waiting for the storm to pass and die down. "I wish I could see Fuji-*san* from the sea," said the Mad Artist. "But I don't think this morning would be the best to try it."

"Nonsense," said Keiji. He walked down over the rocks to where the fishermen sat on their long boats. Approaching the nearest, a weathered man who might have been in his fifties, Keiji spoke, his voice nearly inaudible in the surf.

"This man wishes to see Fuji-*san* from the ocean," said the young samurai, pointing up the rocks at the Mad Artist. "You will take us out on the water."

The weathered man, balding and sun-reddened, shook his head.

"It's too dangerous," he said. "We're going to have a squall, and the squalls bring the *kyoryu*."

Keiji drew his sword and held it to the man's neck, yelling something about insolence as Masaki and the Mad Artist jumped down the piled rocks to stop him.

"Please," said the Mad Artist. "This isn't necessary. I don't need to see her from the water!"

"Why should we change our plans to suit this man's cowardice?" demanded Keiji. "He'll take us to sea, and you'll see Fuji-*san* as Mr. Otojiro wishes."

Mr. Otojiro didn't wish them to see Mt. Fuji from the water. He merely wanted a print depicting her from the coast of Kanagawa. But Keiji didn't care. Even as the fisherman shifted and called his sons (Brothers? They all looked so beaten and old that Masaki couldn't tell) to push the long boat into the water, Keiji stood with his sword out.

"Keiji," said the Mad Artist. "There's no need for this. These men might die. We might die."

"Then we'll die. I won't shrink from it. Mr. Otojiro asked us to do this."

"No he didn't," said Masaki.

Keiji already sat in the boat, bobbing with the fishermen on the water.

"We'll be killed doing this," said the Mad Artist to Masaki. As samurai, Keiji and Masaki had the right to use peasants as they pleased. Today, Keiji wanted his Shikoku, wanted to prove himself a warrior. Watching him sit in the boat, Masaki's heart began to beat quickly, excitement filling him. The ghost of the *kyoryu* scent rose to his nostrils,

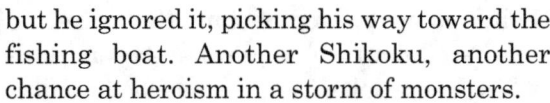

but he ignored it, picking his way toward the fishing boat. Another Shikoku, another chance at heroism in a storm of monsters.

"We can't," said the Mad Artist, following behind the old samurai with reluctance.

The fisherman and his sons rowed out past the place where the high waves washed the rocks. The waves rose around them like blue, snow-capped mountains, Fujis of inconstant water and vaporous spray; cold volcanoes. The real Fuji stood southwest. Masaki had no idea how the Mad Artist would sketch her with the waves and the spray. He suspected the printmaker would do nothing but watch. Either way, Keiji didn't care.

A mile out, the fishermen stopped rowing and let the waves toss their long boat. Keiji stood and paced the deck, but the smell of the *kyoryu* held Masaki. He should have argued with the younger samurai, should not have sat down in the boat. But here they floated, thudding down in the wells of the waves and rising into the air so high it seemed as though everything, even Fuji-*san*, lay below them. "Are you frightened?" Keiji asked the fishermen. None of them answered.

"I've seen enough," the Mad Artist began, but Keiji motioned for him to be quiet.

"Keiji, Mr. Otojiro never asked us to do this," said Masaki. "We must go back to shore."

The smell peaked, and a nest of gray Snake-Necks broke the pitching surface of the sea. White bellies bloomed and retreated underwater; serpentine heads snapped at the fishermen on fifteen foot necks; great flippers buffeted the vessel across the crests of the waves, leaving long barnacle scratches on the hull. The fishy smell of their breath, like whale flesh at the market, blended with the musty *kyoryu* smell in Masaki's head.

Keiji slashed at the necks as they weaved in front of him. A splutter of blood and a sharp-toothed reptilian head fell at Masaki's feet as the body of one of the Snake-Necks sank back into the water. The old samurai drew his sword, but the smell made his sight foggy. Only the cold spray on his face kept him from collapsing.

One of the *kyoryu* struck into the crowd of fishermen, pulling out the oldest of them by his neck. The man screamed as his sons grabbed his arms and legs, trying to hold him in the boat. Masaki struggled to reach them as Keiji swung his sword at the other animals weaving in the surf. The Mad Artist beat with his cane at the Snake-Neck's trunk, trying to make it release the man's head, but it ignored him as it pulled against his sons, tilting the thin boat.

The *kyoryu* turned in the water, pulling the old fisherman away from his sons and over the side. The vessel swayed back and forth as the other Snake-Necks turned on the old man's kicking body. They gulped down chunks of watery flesh like eels or herons. Masaki, too slow to help the old fisherman, watched the bulging lumps of meat move down the creatures' necks.

"Back," he said to the dead man's sons.

The storm broke as they rowed back towards shore, the Mad Artist sobbing and Keiji looking with pride at the severed head of the *kyoryu* lying in the bilge. Masaki could tell he was proud because he sat with an especially straight back, prodding at it with his foot. He had no smile, but pursed his lips like the samurai in paintings. Keiji had killed a man, as Masaki knew he would.

IV: Clear Weather and Brachiosaurs at the Foot of Mt. Fuji

FROM A HILLSIDE in the Sea of Trees, the Mad Artist sketched Fuji-*san*'s red rock slopes and the veins of creeping snow coming from her caldera. Masaki stood by him, beneath a pine tree hung with long vines. In the forest below, a herd of Pine-Eaters tramped through the forest on elephantine legs, crashing through fallen logs and clipping branches with their stubby teeth. They breathed through their foreheads, trumpeting amongst themselves.

Keiji had wandered away to relieve himself. Since the battle at Kanagawa three weeks ago, he said less and less to Masaki

and the Mad Artist. He spent much time practicing with his sword, and kept a few teeth from the *kyoryu* he had killed in his pouch. Today was warm, and it found Masaki thinking about his wife. He never told her about the peasant he killed.

"Are you married?" he asked the Mad Artist.

"I used to be. Now I'm twice a widower," he answered, adding the strong necks of the Pine-Eaters to the wispy trees on his paper.

"Don't you have children to take care of you?" Masaki asked. "Why do you travel around like this, painting and drawing?"

The Mad Artist shrugged.

"I draw things that are dying," he said. "Beautiful things. I have pictures of my wives."

"You draw landscapes," said Masaki. "How can a landscape die?"

"They're always dying," said the Mad Artist. "Fuji-*san* is the only permanent thing I have ever painted, and maybe one day she will be gone."

"But how?" asked Masaki.

The Mad Artist set his brush down and wiped sweat from his bald head.

"Japan has been alone for almost two hundred years. How long do you think that will last? How long can a mere Shogun keep the world away from our tiny islands?"

"As long as necessary," said Masaki, with a twinge of patriotism.

"Necessary? Why is it necessary? Whether the Shogun wants it or not, people already are starting to learn about the foreigners' lands. Our Floating World is beautiful because it will soon be replaced. I paint it because it is gloriously dying."

"I don't believe you," said Masaki.

"All the wonders of the outside will come barreling into us, turning us outward and inward, bottoms upward and heads to the earth. The *kyoryu* won't keep people from the country roads anymore because rich men will put them in zoos or they will die out. People will have no need of printmakers or samurai."

The Mad Artist frowned at his paper, wetted his brush and began to paint again.

"People have no need of samurai now," said Masaki.

"You've kept the Sickle Claws away," said the Mad Artist. With care, he set his drawing on the pine needles of the forest floor to dry and picked up another, clipping a fresh piece of paper to his easel.

"Stand here," said the Mad Artist, motioning with his brush to a spot before his easel.

"Why?"

"I paint things the world should remember," the Mad Artist replied. "Great actors, workers in Edo, Fuji-*san* as she is right now. I haven't done portraits in awhile. I need to practice."

Masaki stepped where bidden. The Mad Artist painted in silence, smiling at some strokes and frowning at others.

"I won't paint Keiji," he said. "The world will see his kind for many years to come."

Perhaps from the herd below, Masaki smelled the rising scent of the *kyoryu*, and felt a famished desire not to be remembered.

V: Storms and Raptors at the Foot of Mt. Fuji

MEN HANGED THEMSELVES in the Sea of Trees, and the Sickle Claws and *haneyube* picked at their bodies. Denied paramours came from the towns around the forest to die in the coolness under the branches. Sometimes, walking in the Sea of Trees, one could find a vertebra or knucklebone in the dirt, bleached as old wood. The woodsmen who worked in the forest would keep these effluvia and play a dice game called "Lover's Leavings," the rules of which differed depending who you asked. Nobody won much from the game, because the woodcutters owned too little to bet their actual property. Instead, they bet things they did not own—Mt. Hiei Temple against the city of Niigata. Hokkaido against Kyushu. The whole world against Mt. Fuji.

Tonight, as lightning sparked around the summit of Fuji-*san*, Masaki stood guard. The Mad Artist and Keiji slept under a shelter made from pine branches. The older samurai

knew that the rain would begin soon, a summer night storm that would cool everything off before turning the forest into a humid and earthy cave, filling the air with a muddy mist.

Everyone said ghosts lived in this forest, and Masaki believed it. Weren't all things just ghosts, the remains of a prior life's lucky kindnesses or pervasive sins? He was a ghost, a ghost who killed other ghosts. Keiji and the Mad Artist were ghosts. The unnamed peasant with the animal eyes and all the *kyoryu* were ghosts.

Tonight he smelled the *kyoryu* scent more strongly than he ever had, a steamy odor that lodged in his skull like an arrowhead. It began when he stood for the Mad Artist and continued long after the sketch of his face was complete. The sketch looked like a ghost's portrait: ragged beard and tired eyes, torn kimono and twisted lips. Masaki had been strangely pleased with it. It looked truer than the image he saw in mirrors and pools of water.

Thunder sounded around Fuji-*san*'s peak. In the silence following it, Masaki heard the same dove-like cooing he had on the shores of Lake Ashi. A shadow stood on the other side of a great pine tree, raising its feathered crest. In the humid lightning, Masaki saw it clearly. The two-tailed Sickle Claw stood before him, its back scarred across the shoulders by the wound Masaki had dealt it over a month ago. It had been eating something—a smudge of blood on its white lips gave it the look of a geisha in makeup.

Masaki drew his sword as he heard clawed feet scurrying in the leaves around the camp. The smell of the *kyoryu* blocked out all the scents of coming rain and pine tar. "Keiji," he said, but he couldn't speak loudly enough. If he yelled, he feared he would vomit. Pointing his sword at the *kyoryu* in front of him, he looked straight into its eyes.

Wide, deep eyes like an animal's. They showed one emotion at a time—triumph to hunger to something like understanding. Masaki felt an exhalation on his neck, and he knew another Sickle Claw stood behind him. He concentrated on the one before him, the

one with two tails and a scarred back. *Kyoryu* were reincarnations, things driven by vengeance or punishment for earthly sins, said the monks. Masaki lowered his sword, stuck it in the mud and knelt before the two-tailed Sickle Claw as it flared its twin peacock fans. The scar on his chest throbbed.

The old samurai opened his kimono, exposing his belly to the *kyoryu*. The claws tore into his stomach—three cuts that loosed his entrails into the brown pine needles. The old scent, the death scent, the smell of the beasts, peaked just before the first downward slash of the great claw, and then dissipated. As he fell, Masaki realized that odor had nothing to do with the *kyoryu*. It was his own smell, the scent of forty years brooding on a young man's crime, an almost human smell.

The *kyoryu* were parodies of men, said the priests, and Masaki agreed. Then he forgot his agreement as he sat up, pushing through something like plaster, kicking his clawed feet, wet with clinging bits of shell and the juice of the egg. Parody could be punishment. He would live as a samurai again, carrying swords on his toes and a topknot of feathers. He would hunt, breed, die and live somewhere else, maybe as a farmer or a soldier or again as a *kyoryu* if one life as such was insufficient repentance. By the time another human bore Masaki, there would be no more samurai. The Mad Artist had been right. But he would also never again be sick with the *kyoryu* scent.

For now, he shrieked for his mother. Far away, two men looked at bloody footprints in the mud and the fallen body of an old samurai. The Mad Artist cried, and Keiji found himself troubled by a strange smell that had haunted him since leaving the shores of Kanagawa. ☉

Hunter C. Eden lives in Nashville and works as a hotelier, writing when his supervisors aren't looking. He recently completed his novel *Mr. Incan Empire,* the touching story of an Aztec mafia battling the reanimated corpse of Charles Darwin on the streets of an alternate Peru.

Interview | BY BILL BAKER

DRAWING UPON THE MASTERS

Legendary comics artist **RICHARD CORBEN** adapts Poe & Lovecraft for Marvel's Haunt of Horror.

Whether you first encountered it in the pages of such classic magazines as *Creepy*, *Eerie*, and *Heavy Metal*, between the covers of such underground comix as *Rowlf* and *Fantagor*, or in any number of graphic novels and collections on the stands today, it's likely that Richard Corben's art left a deep and lasting impression. Combing impeccably rendered human figures and backgrounds, seamless visual storytelling and an unfailing ability to capture the perfect moment and emotion in every panel, Corben's work offers a glimpse into another universe, another reality, and fresh insights into the heart and souls of the beings inhabiting those uncharted realms.

Now, after forty-odd years in the business, Corben has returned to his roots, crafting illustrated versions of choice tales and poems from two seminal authors that readers of this magazine should be intimately familiar with: Edgar Allan Poe and H. P. Lovecraft. Each is highlighted in a volume from Marvel Comics dubbed *Haunt of Horror*.

While it's true that there are a great number of exceptionally fine artists who have successfully delineated the fevered imaginings of Poe and Lovecraft to the comics page, there are few contemporary creators who can equal the adaptations of Richard Corben. This isn't due solely to Corben's gift for realistically portraying the human figure—and particularly the play of emotions on his characters' faces—any more than his ability to render highly detailed backgrounds which possess real weight and exude a palpable atmosphere of ill ease and dread. Rather, it's the artist's affinity for Poe and Lovecraft's visions: an almost genetic comprehension of the very heart and soul of their fearsome verses and tales, which grant his visual realizations their affective power and savage grace.

Corben's creative allies on these books—Richard Margopoulos and Rick Dahl on the Poe volume, and editor Axel Alonzo on both—all prove themselves worthy of the challenge presented them by both their source material and the artist's promethean talent. Another inspired aspect of these projects, the choice to present some of Poe and Lovecraft's lesser-known poems such as "The Lake" and "The Scar" alongside more obvious choices like "The Raven" and "Dagon," allows Corben and his cohorts the opportunity to push both the boundaries of their chosen subject matter and the comics medium itself in new, often unexpected directions.

Thus, radical readings of Eulalie as a sex doll and Izrafel remixed as a rapper appear alongside more traditional interpretations of "The Raven" and "The Tell-Tale Heart." And while Corben cleaves closer to his sources for the Lovecraft outing, he still re-imagines "The Canal" as an allegory for love lost to the horrors of urban life and the power of childhood memory to heal over truths too terrible to comprehend with "The Window."

Inevitably, some of these new versions of Poe and Lovecraft's work won't completely satisfy every reader, as they often take real liberties with their original source material or even defy some of the principal tenets of their originators. Still, all of the adaptations are interesting and entertaining, and most are truly disturbing and discomfiting. Ultimately, *Edgar Allan Poe's Haunt of Horror* and *H. P. Lovecraft's Haunt of Horror* are worthy additions to any aficionado's library of the macabre.

Weird Tales contributor Bill Baker asked Corben to share some background on how the *Haunt* came to be.

How would you describe the Haunt of Horror project, and how did you get involved with it? Axel Alonso, an editor at Marvel and a longtime friend, came up with this brilliant concept. He knew I loved weird horror stories, especially Poe and Lovecraft. He also brought in Rich Margopoulos, who has a keen interest in Poe. I worked with Margopoulos years ago when [Jim] Warren was running many Edgar Allan Poe adaptations in his magazines, *Creepy* and *Eerie*. Rich and I did "The Raven," "The Oval Portrait" and "The Shadow" together—and I have done many projects with Axel at Marvel, and before at DC/Vertigo.

What aspects of Poe's work make it your kind of project? Much of Poe's work deals directly with that most basic of all human feelings, fear, and its more extreme state, horror. He speaks directly to me because I am a very fearful guy. And he expresses these feelings in an artful way, which to me makes them more palatable.

I think my first contact with Poe's work was from the loose movie adaptations that Roger Corman did in the sixties. I was doing commercial art at the time... it never occurred to me that I could do horror comics. Then, when the Warren horror comics started appearing, I felt I had to get into this somehow.

One of the more interesting aspects of the Poe collection is that you and your co-creators largely chose to use his work as inspiration for

OH, LADY DEAR, HAST THOU NO FEAR? WHY AND WHAT ART THOU DREAMING HERE?

SURE THOU ART COME O'ER FAR-OFF SEAS ...

EDGAR ALLAN POE'S HAUNT OF HORROR BY RICHARD CORBEN / MARVEL COMICS

your own, sometimes modernized versions of his tales. What led you folks to take that approach? I think this was an editorial decision. The idea was to have these old stories relate to modern readers. At first I preferred keeping the time period and mood as the author originally wrote it—but now I like them both ways, if the intent and mood is sincere. Margopoulos and Alonso did most of the treatments before I saw them. The only story I wrote for the Poe *Haunt of Horror* was "The Raven," and I kept it roughly in Poe's time frame.

(Actually, with "The Raven," I was trying to recapture the mood and feelings I had when I drew the story years before in *Eerie* magazine, also with Rich Margopoulos. I even drew the same handsome fellow as the lead character. My good friend and fellow comic-book artist Herb Arnold modeled for me in those ancient times.)

It seems like you took a slightly different approach with Lovecraft, not only by handling the scripting yourself, but also by following the original texts more closely. What lead to your taking that approach to adapting Lovecraft's work? When the Poe *Haunt of Horror* was finished we all went on to other projects. Although Axel had mentioned a Lovecraft *Haunt of Horror*, I doubted that it would happen because of other work. There was also some talk of doing more Poe stories, but that didn't happen. When I had time I did some conceptual work for the Lovecraft concept. We didn't want to do the more well-known stories but to adapt some of his interesting poetry. I made a list of stories and poems and brief one-line descriptions of how I would treat them. Based on that, they allowed me to proceed by myself.

In some ways the stories may seem close to the originals, but many Lovecraft fans have objected to the liberties I took. For instance, Lovecraft may have described some unknown frightening threat without telling what it looked like. I felt I had to give this threat an image. Often taking something from the indefinite to the visually real and definite destroys its power. A viewer might realize that the creature really just looks silly rather than unimaginably horrible.

"A tonal image has an automatic harmony, a single=mindedness of vision related to the short story's single=mindedness of thought."

One of the more visually striking things about these books was the choice to present the narrative all in black-and-white and gray tones. What led you to go in that direction? I was in total agreement of producing the books in black-and-white and tones; I wished to evoke the moods of the old black-and-white horror movies. A tonal image has an automatic harmony, a single-mindedness of vision related to the short story's single-mindedness of thought. I hoped I could maintain more control over the pages in tones than in color. Some of the editors also wanted to suggest the era of free-spirited underground comix.

Did you make any new discoveries about these two seminal authors or their work while working on these books? The discoveries I made on these projects were inspired by the other people working with me and seeing their reactions to the material, which were usually quite different than mine. I've read the stories many times, but seeing what another person gets from a story can be a revelation.

You've been doing this for quite some time now. What keeps you making comics through all these years? I have been and am in love with the possibility of comics. I feel the comic artist/author has absolutely as much control over his stories as the text writer has over his. Making visual stories is basic to my purpose in life. To me, reading a good comic is like watching a good movie on paper.

What do you hope your audience gets from your work? Is it all about pure entertainment, or might you hope that they take something a little more substantial away with them? When I'm drawing a comic, I hope for the best. I want the technique to be so correct that it's invisible. Frivolous entertainment is fine and is a good goal to shoot for; sometimes a story has a few more possibilities, and I want to be ready to deliver them. Something about a character, an intriguing plot, an insight to a relationship, about life—you know, heavy stuff.

What's next for you? Will there be new additions to the *Haunt of Horror* line, or have you moved on to something new? Right now I'm

H.P. LOVECRAFT'S HAUNT OF HORROR
BY RICHARD CORBEN / MARVEL COMICS

working on a fantasy adventure for Marvel's [mature-readers] Max line with Daniel Way. Since comic production is dependent on successful business, my feelings about a project may not be the deciding factor. I really enjoyed the *Haunt of Horror* series and would love doing more, but there aren't any plans for additional series right now.

Anything you'd like to add before we let you get back to work? Thanks to everyone who has supported my work over the years. I'll continue to work as hard as I can to make it worthwhile. ☜

For a gallery of classic Corben illustrations, current figure drawings, a checklist of Corben comics, and other projects—from animated movies to special book work—see **www.CorbenStudios.com**.

Lost in Lovecraft

A GUIDED TOUR OF THE DARK MASTER'S WORLD

BY KENNETH HITE

> "*Paradoxically, no spot on earth holds my terrified imagination more potently and breathlessly than the aeon-dead, unknown reaches of the great white antarctic.*"
>
> —H.P. Lovecraft, letter to Robert E. Howard (May 7, 1932)

ANTARCTICA WAS H.P. Lovecraft's first alien world. When he was 10 years old, HPL fell hard for Antarctica and wrote "many fanciful tales about the Antarctic Continent," as he later told his friend Reinhardt Kleiner. What captured Lovecraft's fancy, characteristically enough, was a combination of actual geography (Borchgrevink's 1898-1900 expedition), dime novel (W. Clark Russell's *The Frozen Pirate*, which the eight-year-old HPL devoured), and, most likely, Edgar Allan Poe.

> "*Lost Arctic & Antarctic civilisations form a fascinating idea to me—I used it once in 'Polaris' and expect to use it again more than once.*"
>
> —H.P. Lovecraft, letter to Elizabeth Toldridge (October 25, 1929)

Be that as it may, Lovecraft's first imaginary world was "No-Mans Land," a "vast continent composed of volcanic soil," located at the North Pole. In his juvenile work "The Mysterious Ship," No-Mans Land is the arctic headquarters of a gang of kidnappers, who imprison random individuals there. It is certainly a stretch – but as Lovecraft might say, it is nonetheless darkly suggestive – to connect the polar kidnappers of "The Mysterious Ship" with the Great Race of Yith, who also commit seemingly random kidnappings, likewise removing their victims to inaccessible imprisonment. More suggestive still, the Great Race has its own Arctic connections. For example, according to "The Challenge From Beyond," the cone-beings have "a great polar city" where they stashed the Cube of Yekub. Furthermore, in Lovecraft's original version of "The Shadow Out of Time," the time-napping villains were the men of Lomar in the (not yet) frozen Arctic, the heroes of his early tale "Polaris."

Or so Lovecraft described that draft to Clark Ashton Smith, whose own tales of pre-glacial Hyperborea riffed on the Greek legends of the "land above the North Wind," the home of Apollo. Scholars in Lovecraft's Lomar studied the Pnakotic Manuscripts... which re-emerge four times in At the Mountains of Madness amid discussions of Smith's toad-god Tsathoggua and the Antarctic city of the Old Ones. And what else appears like a mirage in HPL's Antarctic prose? The city of Olathoë, the ancient capital of Lomar, which Dyer describes as a city "of today" beside the "Palaeogaean metropolis" of Antarctica. (I note idly that the entire point of "Polaris" is the impossibility of determining just when, exactly, "today" is.) And Olathoë is very similar to the Old Ones' city: it lies "still and somnolent... on a strange plateau... betwixt strange peaks." It, too, suffers a race war and dies under the ice.

This polar switcheroo puts me in the mind of the Theosophical notion of the "pole shift," in which the Earth (for murky reasons) tumbles on its axis, triggering global catastrophe and racial destruction. If such a pole shift happened some time in the last 26,000 years, Olathoë might well be in Antarctica now! Lovecraft could have discovered the pole shift while swotting up on things Theosophical, but he certainly read about it in Plato and Herodotus, who both mention it obliquely. HPL hints at pole shifting in his collaboration with Robert H. Barlow, "Till A' the Seas," in which the last survivors of the doomed (human) race gather at the South Pole. More polar confusion – or, more precisely, conflation – shows up in "The Dunwich Horror," where we learn of "the inner city at the 2 magnetic poles." Two poles: one city.

"Who can forget the terrible swollen ship poised on the billow-chasm's edge in 'MS. Found in a Bottle'—the dark intimations of her unhallowed age and monstrous growth, her sinister crew of unseeing greybeards, and her frightful southward rush under full sail through the ice of the Antarctic night, sucked onward by some resistless devil-current toward a vortex of eldritch enlightenment which must end in destruction?"

—H.P. Lovecraft, *Supernatural Horror in Literature*

Lovecraft pole-shifts (and Poe-shifts) in *Mountains*, when he equates Poe's "Mount Yaanek in the realms of the boreal [north] pole" (from "Ulalume") with Mount Erebus in Antarctica. In his own novel The Narrative of Arthur Gordon Pym, Poe likewise shifts his poles, rotating the North Polar "Hyperborean" myth—of a warm land beyond the wind—south to Antarctica. But instead of literally Apollonian gods, Poe populates the black island of Tsalal (his anti-Hyperborea) with Dionysian savages, prone to panic and murder. This attribution of malignity to the Antarctic seems original with Poe, for all that the medieval geographers populated the "Antipodes" and "Terra Incognita Australis" with grotesques. Before Poe, for example, Coleridge's castaway in "The Rime of the Ancient Mariner" discovers a benevolent Spirit in the far reaches of the southern sea. In Moby-Dick, Melville follows Poe, with a supernaturally white death-bringer from the Antarctic oceans. Regardless of how they charge their poles, though, Coleridge, Poe, and Melville all end their narratives in maelstrom.

"Danforth was a great reader of bizarre material, and had talked a good deal of Poe. I was interested myself because of the antarctic scene of Poe's only long story—the disturbing and enigmatical Arthur Gordon Pym."

—H.P. Lovecraft, *At the Mountains of Madness*

Lovecraft's Antarctic voyage, his "remake" of Pym, also ends in a maelstrom, albeit an intellectual one. Both Pym and Mountains begin in dry, almost clinical terms: Poe's sea narrative and Lovecraft's scientific report. But soon enough, disaster strikes; race

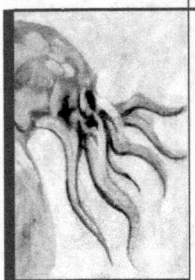

war tears apart Pym's ship, and the Old Ones kill Dyer's fellow scientists. Both Pym and Dyer pass through a series of descents to discover strange hieroglyphics and a mysterious half-seen figure of terror. Both sets of hieroglyphics are disturbingly cosmic: Poe's are startlingly large, comprising entire passageways, while Lovecraft's are unthinkably ancient. And, of course, Lovecraft explicitly tips his hat to Poe by transferring the cry of "Tekeli-li! Tekeli-li!" from the eerie white birds of Tsalal to the bubbling black shoggoth of Kadath. (One can distract oneself endlessly hunting for the original source of that cry: I find Poe scholar J.V. Ridgely's theory, deriving it from the Maori tekelili, "to shiver or shake," pretty convincing.) But where Poe is writing a journey of the psyche, purified by horrors and exalted by the discovery of its Source at the end of the world, Lovecraft is telling a journey of the intellect, battered by discoveries and horrified by its Source at the beginning of the world.

"That the antarctic continent was once temperate and even tropical, with a teeming vegetable and animal life of which the lichens, marine fauna, arachnida, and penguins of the northern edge are the only survivals, is a matter of common information; and we hoped to expand that information in variety, accuracy, and detail."

—H.P. Lovecraft, *At the Mountains of Madness*

Robert M. Price famously pinpoints *Mountains* as the high water mark of Lovecraft's "demythologization" of his own cosmos. In its pages, the Necronomicon stands revealed as medieval distortion and cultist raving, and the Pnakotic Manuscripts become simply tumbled accretions around half-understood alien detritus. Mighty Cthulhu is but one member of a transient species of octopoid aliens, and Tsathoggua just a broken memory of the Old Ones. Fabled Leng becomes a name attached by mystics to the Old Ones' plateau, and "Kadath in the Cold

> *Both Poe's and Lovecraft's protags descend past strange hieroglyphics to discover a half-seen figure of terror.*

Waste," far from being the mountain of the gods it was in its eponymous Dream-Quest, is only the tumbled ruins of the Old Ones' slave pen. Mythology becomes paleontology; archaeology takes the place of mysticism. There is no blasphemous knowledge; there are no gods to be blasphemed. Antarctica is neither the fecund womb of Poe's Gnostic imagination nor the soul-erasing vortex of his Gothic fears, but merely an icy Petri dish left in untidy condition by vegetable-men from another world.

"In the whole spectacle there was a persistent, pervasive hint of stupendous secrecy and potential revelation. It was as if these stark, nightmare spires marked the pylons of a frightful gateway into forbidden spheres of dream, and complex gulfs of remote time, space, and ultra-dimensionality. I could not help feeling that they were evil things—mountains of madness whose farther slopes looked out over some accursed ultimate abyss. That seething, half-luminous cloud background held ineffable suggestions of a vague, ethereal beyondness far more than terrestrially spatial, and gave appalling reminders of the utter remoteness, separateness, desolation, and aeon-long death of this untrodden and unfathomed austral world."

—H.P. Lovecraft, *At the Mountains of Madness*

Certainly Price is correct, on the surface, at least as far as Dyer knows and tells us. But for such a rigorous demythologizer, Dyer has a strong streak of Arthur Gordon Pym in him. His quote above certainly doesn't sound like a geologist's report. It sounds, rather, like the ravings of a mystic, or (Poe might suggest) of an initiate. Lovecraft doesn't "demythologize" his cosmos in Mountains; if anything, he remythologizes Antarctica—and by extension, our cosmos—in that novel. Antarctica—"the strangest, weirdest, and most terrible of all the corners of earth's globe"—becomes another world, a world of Lovecraftian mystery. Lake's transmission compares Antarctica to a "land of mystery in a dream," or a "gateway" to a "forbidden world of untrodden wonder." Dyer goes even farther, calling it the "unknown antarctic world of disordered time and alien natural law." Those "mountains of madness," which are "a frightful gateway into forbidden spheres of dream," are nothing compared to the range beyond, which are "the focus of the world's evil," and seem like "the serrated edge of a monstrous alien planet," for example.

Having read Dyer's warning, we see Antarctica anew through Lovecraft's eyes. Every expedition's report becomes fodder for his new mythology. Just lately, for example, paleontologists have determined that all octopi share a single Antarctic ancestor, and geologists have discovered an unknown mountain range buried beneath the Antarctic ice sheet in defiance of all known rules of plate tectonics. We read such news from the bottom of the world, and shudder. Perhaps Lovecraft knew best, when he wrote in the sonnet "Antarktos": "the bird told of vaster parts, that under / The mile-deep ice-shroud crouch and brood and bide." Under the scientific mind, frozen in place by human hubris, bigger truths "crouch and brood and bide." A truth "very far larger in its proportions," as Arthur Gordon Pym says, "than any dweller among men." Tekeli-li! Tekeli-li! ☉

Next Stop on the Tour: *Antiquity*

The Cryptic

M.R. JAMES & HIS PLEASING TERRORS

I'VE HAD THE privilege of seeing Montague Rhodes James in person twice now—or at least as close as is possible to attend upon a man who shuffled off this mortal coil in 1936. It isn't surprising, I suppose, that James, who ranks among the 20th century's leading describers of things that don't stay dead, should have been brought back to life before my eyes. In this instance, it was done by an extremely talented English actor named Robert Lloyd Parry, who appears on the stage in Edwardian garb, surrounded by minimal furniture and such small props as may become relevant: a glass and decanter, a few books, perhaps what seems to be an ancient manuscript. He then tells—or recites and partially acts out—stories by James. It's a very sophisticated illusion, giving the impression of James himself before us, declaiming his stories and in turn assuming the role of his beleaguered protagonists.

So far I have seen Mr. Parry perform four stories: "Canon Alberic's Scrapbook," "The Mezzotint," "Oh, Whistle, and I'll Come to You My Lad," and "The Ash Tree." He groups them as two different shows, the first called "A Pleasing Terror" and the second, "Oh, Whistle..." I saw the first at the 2007 World Fantasy Convention in Saratoga Springs, New York, where I was chairman of programming and the convention's theme was "Ghosts and Revenants." Under the circumstances, when a well-reviewed professional actor offered to put on such a performance, it was like being handed gold on a platter. I would have to have been an idiot to refuse.

I came early, to make sure I'd get a seat at all. As it turned out, there were about three seats for everyone in attendance, as most con-goers were at the evening's parties. The more fool them: they missed something spectacular. While it is a general rule that you should never pass up a live theatrical event at a World Fantasy Convention because they are rare and special occurrences, this one succeeded beyond my wildest expectations.

"...brilliant," I heard Christopher Roden remark. Roden and his wife Barbara publish Ash-Tree Press, and are both among the world's leading experts in all things Jamesian. That he used a modifier of which James himself would certainly not approve may be attributed to the difference between our time and James's, and the kind of amazed enthusiasm a Parry performance can arouse in a knowledgeable audience. Needless to say, when I had a chance to see Mr. Parry again, in New York, performing "Oh, Whistle..." at the 78th Street Theatre Lab under the auspices of The Open Book—a readers' theatre company founded in 1975 by Bill Bonham and Marvin Kaye—I of course jumped at the opportunity. The show will be gone by the time you read this, but if you should ever, anywhere, get the chance to see Robert Lloyd Parry doing M.R. James, go. Meanwhile, you can see brief clips of him online at **http://uk.youtube.com/user/NunkieTheatreUSA.** No filmed version of his performances seems to be generally available. I can't help but feel that the experience of watching him on the screen, however impressive that might be, would not quite have the same power as see-

76 ~ WEIRD TALES ~ Spring 2009

ing and hearing him in person, in a small, closed room. But you have to make do with what you can get. A filmed version, if it ever becomes available, will be a must for any fan of the ghostly and terrible.

Who was M.R. James? Those of you who don't yet know have a wonderful discovery ahead of you. Certainly for anyone who aspires to write supernatural fiction, it is an essential discovery and part of one's artistic growth. I don't suggest that you have to go through a phase of writing James pastiches, but he is one of those writers, like Lovecraft and Poe, with whom the entire field is engaged in an ongoing dialogue. The book you want is simply called *The Collected Ghost Stories of M.R. James*, first published in 1931 and reprinted endlessly since. (Or, if you are inclined to luxury, you can try to find the Ash-Tree Press version, *A Pleasing Terror*, put out by the Rodens, which is definitive, annotated, and contains much material not in *The Collected Ghost Stories*, including two extra stories, some fragments, a play, the entire text of James's rare juvenile novel *The Five Jars*, and several very good appendices and articles. Unfortunately, it is out of print at the moment and likely to be expensive.)

H.P. Lovecraft ranked James among the four "Modern Masters" (along with Algernon Blackwood, Arthur Machen, and Lord Dunsany) in his seminal essay, "Supernatural Horror in Literature." Of James he wrote: "...gifted with an almost diabolic power of calling horror by gentle steps from the midst of prosaic daily life, is the scholarly Montague Rhodes James, Provost of Eton College, antiquary of note, and recognized authority on medieval manuscripts and cathedral history. Dr. James, long fond of telling spectral tales at Christmastide, has become by slow degrees a literary weird fictionist of the very first rank; and has developed a distinctive style and method likely to serve as models for an enduring line of disciples."

This last observation proved prophetic. James did indeed develop a whole school of disciples, jokingly referred to by connoisseurs as "The James Gang," many of whose works you can find in print from Ash-Tree Press. His influence has also extended more generally, to writers like Ramsey Campbell, who cites him as a favorite, and to the late Charles Grant and his entire school of "quiet" horror, as typified by his own work and his celebrated *Shadows* anthologies, all of which have their roots in James.

James's fiction represented a distinct aesthetic of the ghost story. The typical James story is about an English scholar on holiday, visiting some remote district, who investigates a quaint church or ruin, acquires a ancient artifact (such as a manuscript, or, in one famous instance, a whistle), or otherwise manages to stir up something, either the spirit of a dead person, or some elemental force, which would be best left alone. Supernatural manifestations are usually, except sometimes at the climax, barely glimpsed, though their presence is strongly felt. There is something against a window which might be a seagull's wing, or might not be. A character slides his hand under a pillow and realizes he's placed it in a mouth. The hero of "Canon Alberic's Scrapbook," studying that precious medieval tome—which he has acquired for an impossibly low sum from a gentleman entirely too eager to get rid of it—seated in his half-darkened room, suddenly realizes that the thing on the table beside him is not a dust-mop or a crumpled rag, but an inhuman, hairy claw.

James had very exact ideas about how a ghost story should work and what it should be. He wrote several essays on the subject, most notably "Some Remarks on Ghost Stories" (1929). Unsurprisingly, his "rules" for the ideal ghost story most accurately describe his own work. This is always the case. Critical "theories" tend to be retrospective and descriptive, quite unlike scientific ones. The "evidence" they are based on comes from what has already been written. When the theory is produced by an actual practitioner, it tends to explain that writer's work.

Whether it applies more generally is problematic. Raymond Chandler's "The Simple Art of Murder" will tell you a great deal about how to write a Raymond Chandler mystery story, but not a lot about, say, Arthur Conan Doyle. Hemingway on the realistic novel will tell you much about Hemingway and this methods. Lovecraft letters and essays on cosmic horror will illuminate Lovecraft, whose approach and aesthetics were similar to James in some ways, but profoundly different in others. Tolkien's "On Fairy Stories" reveals Tolkien's inner workings, but not necessarily anything that applies to the fantasy fiction of, say, China Mieville. Other writers can take away some useful bits, but critical theories are never hard-and-fast formulas, much less the literary equivalent of paint-by-numbers.

James knew this. Using a typical, elegantly-turned phrase, he remarked that he was listing "characteristics observed to accompany success." A few of his standards, we can, today, dismiss outright. It was entirely appropriate for an Eton provost who began telling ghost stories to the Chitchat Club in 1893 to conclude that sex had no place in the ghost story. Today, standards have changed. The supernatural story with eroticism out in the open has been a distinct type since the days of Clark Ashton Smith and early C.L. Moore, not to mention such masterpieces as Fritz Leiber's "The Girl with the Hungry Eyes." Maybe the flurry of *Hot Blood*-type anthologies carried the possibilities a bit too far at times, but the erotic horror story is here to stay.

Nevertheless, we should still pay attention to James. He is wiser than he immediately lets on. He was perhaps too modest to claim any philosophical importance for ghost stories. Their purpose, he wrote, was to amuse, "with the sole object of inspiring a pleasing terror in the reader," adding: "If they do so, well; but, if not, let us regulate them to the top shelf and say no more about it."

Within his chosen limitations, James definitely knew his stuff. To achieve "pleasing terror," he insisted, the ghost or spectral manifestation had to be, first and foremost, malevolent. The next thing required was "reticence." He strongly disapproved of the unsubtle, the gross, and the crude, condemning more than once Christine Campbell Thompson's *Not At Night* series of anthologies, which were actually British, though he believed them to be American because much of the contents was drawn from early issues of *Weird Tales*. "Of course, all writers of ghost stories do desire to make their readers' flesh creep," he wrote, "but these are shameless in their attempts. They are unbelievably crude and sudden, and they wallow in corruption."

If James ever read any Lovecraft, it was "The Horror At Red Hook"—not a fortunate choice, and far from Lovecraft's best. The irony is that Lovecraft would have agreed with most of James's disparaging comments, even about his own work.

It would be simplistic to suggest that James was merely being a prude. The candid truth of the matter is that he was a lot more sophisticated and subtle than the pulp writers he encountered in the *Not At Night* books; but this does not mean his stories were polite and delicate to the point of vitiation. A good James story, as someone put it once, could scare a week-old corpse. His work contains images, very difficult to dismiss from the memory, such as the doomed victim hideously bouncing up and down in bed in an inexplicable manner in "The Ash-Tree" as a result of (we later learn) being bitten to death by enormous spiders spawned from the grave of a witch. It's likewise hard to forget that perfect phrase in "The Haunted Doll's House," in which, glimpsed from afar, a hairy, toadlike thing causes the deaths of two small children: "It was busy about the truckle-beds, but not for long."

James further advised that setting was an immensely important aspect of a ghost story, since the number of things a ghost can actually do (seek revenge, demand justice, reveal hidden secrets) are rather limited.

ILLUSTRATION BY ZULLA

Being as he was an expert in cathedrals and church architecture and an enthusiastic tourist to some of the more out-of-the-way parts of England and the neighboring countries, his stories tend to be set in carefully-described remote villages, half-forgotten country churches, or in similarly obscure parts of France, or in the case of the famous "Count Magnus," Sweden. In this, he has something in common with Lovecraft. Both believed that the setting should be made as convincing as possible, with deft use of prosaic details, to maintain plausibility once the fantastic element begins to intrude.

Another key element is *intrusion*. All James's stories are about something frightening and fantastic gradually breaking into the everyday world—although in James, as opposed to Lovecraft, it is not a matter of cosmic horrors from beyond the Earth, but something that is better left undisturbed, a potent remnant of the past that won't stay dead.

In order to keep up that prosaic sense of reality, James recommended that the story should not be set very far in the past: maybe a couple generations back, but not so far as to seem fantastic and remote. "Anything, we feel, might have happened in the fifteenth century," he wrote in "Some Remarks on Ghost Stories," adding that "The seer of ghosts must talk something like me, and be dressed, if not in my fashion, yet not too much like a man in a pageant, if he is to enlist my sympathy."

Some of you may be impatiently compiling a list of classic stories that break every last one of the James "rules." It is possible to set a good ghost or supernatural story in the remote historical past. More familiar settings may still work better. It would be easier to set a ghostly story in the Rome of the Caesars than in Ur of the Chaldees, the latter could be done. It would be possible to set such a story among cave men in the Ice Age. It is certainly possible, as everyone from Robert E. Howard to Tolkien proved, to place one in an entirely fabulous landscape. Clark Ashton Smith did them both one better and set such stories in the remote future, on the Earth's last continent of Zothique, or even on other planets. As I've already mentioned, the supernatural horror story with a substantial erotic element is now a commonplace.

Not every such story needs to be reticent either. We may also observe the success of stories which are loud and completely up-front, not creeping slowly into the reader's sensibilities but socking him powerfully between the eyes on page one. Regardless of what one thinks of the short-lived splatterpunk trend, it's undeniable that Harlan Ellison wrote such stories for decades before anybody proclaimed it a movement. David Schow, Joe R. Lansdale, Clive Barker, and numerous others have also done so. They wouldn't have met M.R. James's approval, but theirs are still powerful stories, often put together with considerable artistry.

I return to the observation that when a practitioner ventures into critical theory, he ends up describing his own work. Certainly James describe a method for writing a very effective ghost story. He himself put it into practice brilliantly. His followers did it with varying degrees of brilliance or lack thereof. The reason that, more than a hundred years on, his stories are still potent and that an actor like Robert Lloyd Parry can make first-rate theatrical performances out of them is because the Jamesian method—rule-book, formula, or whatever you want to call it—still works. Readers will continue to enjoy these stories for a long time to come. Writers will continue to learn from them.

James continues to haunt us. His terrors remain pleasing. They do not have to be relegated to the upper shelf. We will continue to say a good deal about them. ❧

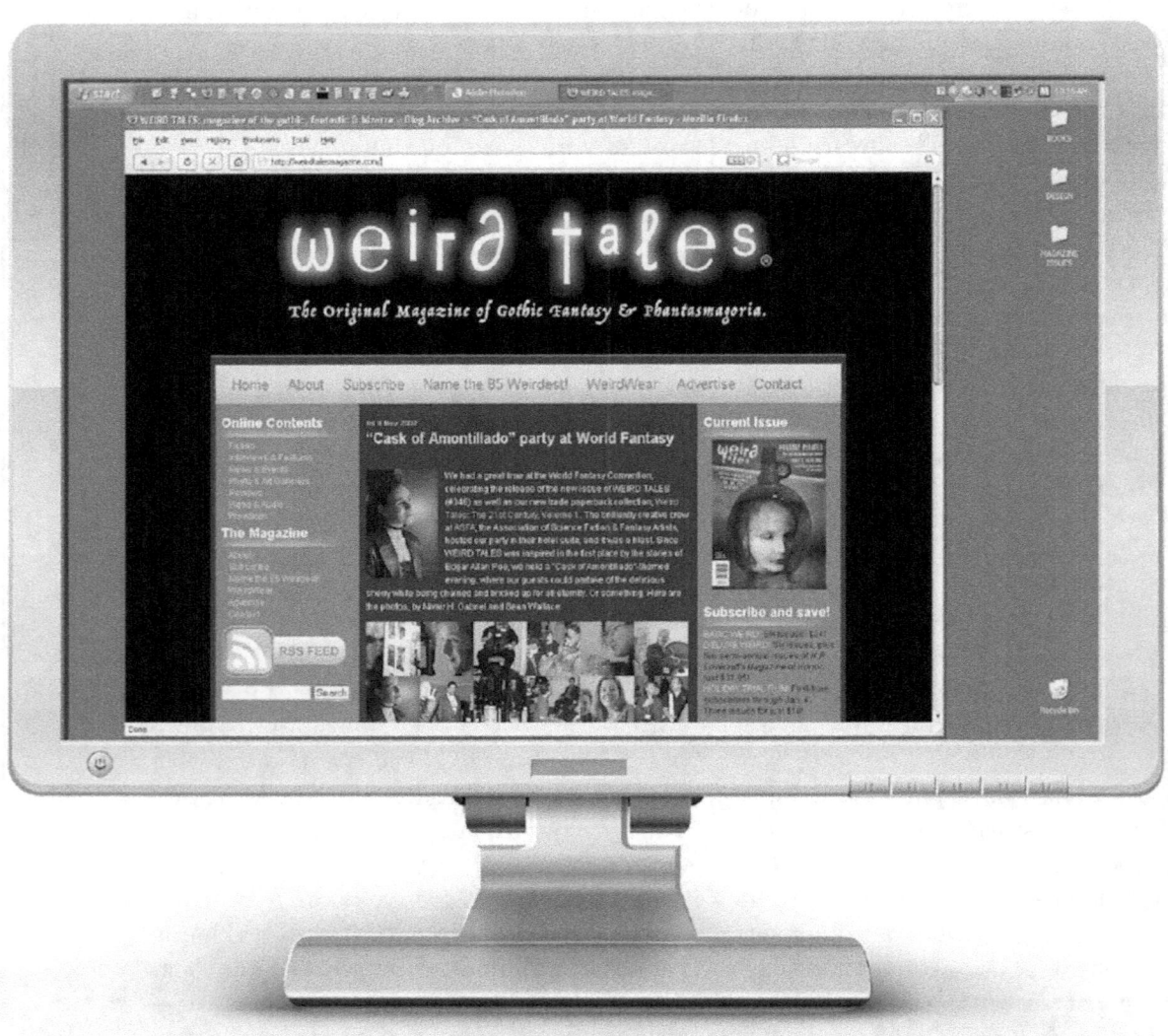